"This complex novel—scathing ... inspiring—constructs a seductive puzzle from torn identities, focusing on both the value and peril of fear. . . . Gregory's beautiful imagery and metaphors bring bittersweet intimacy and tenderness to the primal wonder of star-lit legends. Isolated people, both victims and victimizers, are ghosts in a waking world, blind to their encounters with living nightmares. Blending the stark realism of pain and isolation with the liberating force of the fantastic, Gregory (*Afterparty*) makes it easy to believe that the world is an illusion, behind which lurks an alternative truth—dark, degenerate, and sublime."
—*Publishers Weekly*, starred review

"A superb, haunting tale by one of our very best writers. Gregory's characters are already in therapy; you may want to join them after reading this spicy, disturbing mélange."
—Robert J. Sawyer, Hugo Award–winning author of *Red Planet Blues*

"Clever, and filled with the creeping dread of what's in the flickering shadow next to you and what's just around the corner that suffuses the best horror. I loved it."
—Ellen Datlow, World Fantasy and International Horror Guild award-winning editor of *The Best Horror of the Year* series

"Charming and horrifying—you won't be able to stop reading it."
—Tim Powers, award-winning author of *Declare* and *The Stress of Her Regard*

"Daryl Gregory is a writer I would happily follow into any dark place he wanted me to go. This is a labyrinth of a story, intricate

as a spider's web—and like a spider's web, each piece informs the whole. Beautiful."
—Seanan McGuire, author of the October Daye series and *Half-Off Ragnarok*

Praise for Daryl Gregory

"A bright new voice of the twenty-first century. . . ."
—*Library Journal*

"A quietly brilliant second novel. . . . A wide variety of believable characters, a well-developed sense of place and some fascinating scientific speculation."
—*Publishers Weekly,* starred review (on *The Devil's Alphabet*)

"Compelling and creepy . . . evokes the best of Stephen King."
—*Kirkus* (on *The Devil's Alphabet*)

"Part superhero fiction, part zombie horror story, and part supernatural thriller, this luminous and compelling tale deserves a wide readership beyond genre fans."
—*Library Journal,* starred review (on *Raising Stony Mayhall*)

"More than many novelists, Gregory's work not only withstands but grows richer with re-readings and sustained attention."
—*SF Signal*

WE ARE ALL COMPLETELY FINE

DARYL GREGORY

TACHYON | SAN FRANCISCO

Cover and interior design by Elizabeth Story

Tachyon Publications
1459 18th Street #139
San Francisco, CA 94107
(415) 285-5615
tachyon@tachyonpublications.com

www.tachyonpublications.com
smart science fiction & fantasy

Series Editor: Jacob Weisman
Project Editor: Jill Roberts

ISBN 13: 978-1-61696-171-8
ISBN 10: 1-61696-171-6

Printed in the United States of America by Worzalla

First Edition: 2014
9 8 7 6 5 4 3 2 1

Acknowledgments

This story couldn't have been written without Dr. Kathleen Bieschke, psychologist, expert therapist, and my beta reader since Day One. Did I also mention that she's my lovely wife? Years ago Kath turned me on to the novels of Irvin Yalom, who in his day job is the world's leading expert on small groups. He wrote the bible on the subject, *The Theory and Practice of Group Psychotherapy*, which I read and reread while writing this novella. Anything here that makes Bieschke, Yalom, et al. (et al. to include the alarming number of shrinks I hang out with) cringe or shake their heads is no fault of theirs. They tried to educate me, but some patients are resistant to change.

Thanks as well to my own small group of fellow-sufferers, the writers who read and commented on this book: Gary Delafield, Jack Skillingstead, Nancy Kress, and Dave Justus. Some day we'll kick this thing.

And to Jacob, Jill, and the fine folks at Tachyon: you're the best enablers ever!

For Jill Morgan and Bob Slaney

Chapter 1

There were six of us in the beginning. Three men and two women, and Dr. Sayer. *Jan,* though some of us never learned to call her by her first name. She was the psychologist who found us, then persuaded us that a group experience could prove useful in ways that one-on-one counseling could not. After all, one of the issues we had in common was that we each thought we were unique. Not just survivors, but *sole* survivors. We wore our scars like badges.

Consider Harrison, one of the first of us to arrive at the building for that initial meeting. Once upon a time he'd been the Boy Hero of Dunnsmouth. The Monster Detective. Now he sat behind the wheel of his car, watching the windows of her office, trying to decide whether he would break his promise to her and skip out. The office was in a two-story, Craft-style house on the north side of the city, on a woodsy block that could look sinister or comforting depending on the light. A decade before, this family home had been rezoned and colonized by shrinks; they converted the bedrooms to offices, made the living room into a lobby, and planted a sign out front declaring its name to be "The Elms." Maybe not the best name, Harrison thought. He would have suggested a species of tree that wasn't constantly in danger of being wiped out.

Today, the street did not look sinister. It was a sunny spring day, one of the few tolerable days the city would get before the heat and humidity rolled in for the summer. So why ruin it with ninety minutes of self-pity and communal humiliation?

He was suspicious of the very premise of therapy. The idea that people could change themselves, he told Dr. Sayer in their pre-group interview, was a self-serving delusion. She believed that people were captains of their own destiny. He agreed, as long as it was understood that every captain was destined to go down with the ship, and there wasn't a damned thing you could do about it. If you want to stand there with the wheel in your hand and pretend you were steering, he told her, knock yourself out.

She'd said, "Yet you're here."

He shrugged. "I have trouble sleeping. My psychiatrist said he wouldn't renew my prescriptions unless I tried therapy."

"Is that all?"

"Also, I might be *entertaining* the idea of tamping down my nihilism. Just a bit. Not because life is *not* meaningless—I think that's inarguable. It's just that the constant awareness of its pointlessness is exhausting. I wouldn't mind being oblivious again. I'd love to feel the wind in my face and think, just for minute, that I'm not going to crash into the rocks."

"You're saying you'd like to be happy."

"Yeah. That."

She smiled. He liked that smile. "Promise me you'll try one meeting," she said. "Just give me one."

Now he was having second thoughts. It wasn't too late to drive away. He could always find a new psychiatrist to fork over the meds.

A blue and white transit van pulled into the handicap parking spot in front of the house. The driver hopped out. He was a hefty white kid, over six feet tall with a scruffy beard, dressed in the half-ass uniform of the retail class: colored polo over Gap khakis. He opened the rearmost door of the van to reveal an old man waiting in a wheelchair.

The driver thumbed a control box, and the lift lowered the chair and occupant to the ground with the robotic slow motion of a space shuttle arm. The old man was already half astronaut, with his breathing mask and plastic tubes and tanks of onboard oxygen. His hands seemed to be covered by mittens.

Was this geezer part of the group, Harrison wondered, or visiting some other shrink in the building? Just how damaged were the people that Dr. Sayer had recruited? He had no desire to spend hours with the last people voted off Victim Island.

The driver seemed to have no patience for his patient. Instead of going the long way around to the ramp, he pushed the old man to the curb, then roughly tilted him back—too far back—and bounced the front wheels down on the sidewalk. The old man pressed his mittened hands to his face, trying to keep the mask in place. Another series of heaves and jerks got the man up the short stairs and into the house.

Then Harrison noticed the girl. Eighteen, maybe nineteen years old, sitting on a bench across from the house, watching the old man and the driver intently. She wore a black, long-sleeved T-shirt, black jeans, black Chuck Taylors: the Standard Goth Burka. Her short white hair looked like it had been not so much styled as attacked. Her hands gripped the edge of the bench and she did not relax even after the pair had gone inside. She was like a feral cat: skinny, glint-eyed, shock-haired. Ready to bolt.

For the next few minutes he watched the girl as she watched the front of the house. A few people passed by on the sidewalk, and then a tall white woman stepped up to the door. Fortyish, with careful hair and a Hillary Clinton pantsuit. She moved with an air of concentration; when she climbed the steps, she placed each foot carefully, as if testing the solidity of each surface.

A black guy in flannels and thick work boots clumped up the stairs behind the woman. She stopped, turned. The guy looked up at the roof of the porch. An odd thing. He carried a backpack and wore thick black sunglasses, and Harrison couldn't imagine what he saw up there. The white woman said something to him, holding open the door, and he nodded. They went inside together.

It was almost six o'clock, so Harrison assumed that everyone who'd gone in was part of the group. The girl, though, still hadn't made a move toward the door.

"Fuck it," Harrison said. He got out of the car before he could change his mind, and then walked toward the house. When he reached the front sidewalk he glanced behind him—casually, casually. The girl noticed him and looked away. He was certain that she'd been invited to the group too. He was willing to bet that she might be the craziest one of all.

The van driver was walking out as Harrison was walking in. Harrison nodded at him—or rather, gave him what he thought of as the *bro nod*, that upward tip of the chin that American men used to acknowledge each other. The driver frowned as if this were some breach of protocol.

So, Harrison thought, the driver was an asshole to everybody, not just his riders.

Dr. Sayer was standing outside a room on the ground floor of the house, like a teacher welcoming students on their first day. She was dressed like a teacher, too, in a sweater and skirt, though Harrison towered over her. She was barely over five feet tall, with skinny arms and toned legs, but a surprisingly stocky torso. He thought of several unkind comparisons—Mrs. Potato Head, or a cartoon M&M—and was happy she couldn't read his thoughts.

"Harrison," she said. "I'm so glad you came. Is everything all right?"

"I'm fine." What had she seen in his face? His judgment of her? His annoyance with the driver? He'd have to watch himself with the doctor. Maybe with the whole group. "I told you I'd come, so I'm here."

His tone was still too sharp, but Dr. Sayer let it pass. "Go ahead and take a seat," she said, indicating the room. When Harrison had met with her before, it was upstairs, in what he took to be her usual office. He supposed she needed a bigger room for the group. "We'll start in a few minutes," she said.

He hesitated, and she tilted her head questioningly.

He thought about telling her about the girl outside, then thought better of it. "Okay," he said. "See you on the other side."

The three people he'd spotted entering the house were seated on one side of the circle. The man in the wheelchair had lowered his mask. Harrison realized with a start that the man had no hands; the arms ended below the elbow and were covered by what looked like white athletic socks.

Harrison raised a hand in greeting—and immediately felt self-conscious. Look, *I* have hands.

"Hi there," the old man said. The woman in the pantsuit smiled warmly.

The guy in the sunglasses seemed not to notice him from behind those shades. He was only in his twenties, Harrison realized. Maybe as young as the girl outside.

There were six chairs, including the wheelchair. A notebook and pen sat on one, reserving it for Dr. Sayer. The only two spots remaining had their back to the door, one next to the doctor's seat, across from Stevie Wonder. The other was next to Ironside—and he couldn't choose the one not next to the disabled guy without looking like a dick. "I'm Stan," the old man said.

Before Harrison could answer, the man in the glasses said, "I think we should wait."

Stan said, "For what?"

"Until everyone gets here."

Harrison turned to Stan. "I'm Harrison."

The woman glanced at the man in the sunglasses, hesitated.

"And you are?" Harrison asked the woman.

She seemed embarrassed. "I'm Barbara."

Harrison extended a hand. "Nice to meet you, Barbara."

Mr. Sunglasses opened his mouth, then shut it. That silenced everyone for several minutes. The fifth seat—sixth counting Stan's wheelchair—remained empty.

This room, Harrison guessed, had once been the sunroom of the house, and before that, an open porch. The psychologists had done their best to disguise this, laying down rugs and hiding many of the windows behind Roman shades, but there was still too much naked glass for a private therapy group. Outside was a small backyard walled by arborvitaes. A peeping tom would have no trouble hiding back there. He wondered if the doctors had thought this through. And then he wondered what the collective noun was for psychologists: a shortage of shrinks? A confession of counselors?

Dr. Sayer came into the room. "I think this may be it for today." She picked up her notebook and sat down.

"Were you waiting for a blonde woman?" Harrison

asked. Everyone looked at him. "I saw someone outside."

Dr. Sayer thought for a moment, then looked at her wristwatch. Harrison thought, Of course she's a clock watcher. A requisite characteristic for the profession.

"I think we should get started," she said. "First, call me Jan. Some of you have known me for over a year, but some of you I've only recently met. We've all talked individually about why you might find this group useful. Each of you has had experiences that have been discounted by other therapists. Sometimes your friends and family don't believe what happened to you. Many of you have decided, reasonably enough, that it's not safe talking about your experiences. This group is that safe place. We've all agreed that what is said here stays in the strictest confidence."

No one spoke. Harrison stole a glance at the others, and they were all concentrating on the doctor.

"Think of this place as a lab," said the doctor—*Jan*. "You can experiment with honesty, with sharing your feelings, even really negative feelings. If you try that out in the real world—well, watch out. Feelings get hurt, there are misunderstandings—"

"You end up in the loony bin," Stan said.

Jan smiled. "But here, it's your job to give real feedback, and to take it. There's no other place where you can be so honest, yet still have people show up every week."

"A dinner party for gluttons for punishment," Harrison said.

No one laughed. *Uh oh,* he thought.

"Why don't we go around the room and introduce ourselves," she said.

"They already started," the man in the sunglasses said to the doctor. "Introducing themselves."

"That's understandable," Jan said.

"My name is Stan." The old man coughed hard and then cleared his throat. "You probably already know who I am—can't hide these stumps." He grinned, and his teeth seemed too big and too white. "So . . . yes. I'm the man who survived the Weaver family."

Harrison thought the man's age was about right for that. Barbara, to Stan's left, nodded. The man in the sunglasses said, "I'm sorry, who?"

Stan twisted in his chair. "The *Weavers*," he said, louder. Still Mr. Sunglasses didn't respond. "The Arkansas Cannibals?"

"Never heard of them."

Stan looked exasperated. "The Spider Folk?"

"That was a long time ago," Harrison said. "He may be too young."

"1974! And you're as young as he is," Stan said. Harrison thought, no, actually. The sunglasses man was probably five or ten years younger than Harrison, mid-twenties maybe, though that pudgy body made him look older. Or maybe Stan just couldn't judge the age of black people.

Stan mumbled something and pushed the oxygen mask to his face.

"I'm sorry," Mr. Sunglasses said. "I just don't—"

"It was the biggest story of the year," Stan said. He'd pulled down the mask again. "I was on *Merv Griffin*."

"Maybe you should go next," Harrison said to the man in the glasses. He still hadn't taken them off, despite how dark and bulky they looked. They looked more functional than fashionable. Was he blind? Maybe Harrison should be nicer to him. After too long a pause, Harrison added, "If you don't mind."

The request seemed to flummox the sunglasses man. "She's next to him," he said, indicating Barbara. "It's not my turn."

"Oh, I can go," she said.

Harrison looked at the man in sunglasses and thought, Really? You need to go in *order*?

Something must have shown on Harrison's face, because the man said, "My name is Martin."

"Hello, Martin," Barbara said. She held out her hand, and he took it hesitantly.

"Do you want me to talk about my history?" Martin asked Jan. "Why I'm here?"

"Whatever you're comfortable with," the doctor said. "You can—"

Martin jerked in his chair. He was looking over Jan's shoulder with an expression of shock. The doctor turned.

The blonde girl stood in the doorway. She seemed to feel the group's gaze like a harsh light. She endured it for a moment, then walked into the room, eyes down and face closed, and took the last seat, between Harrison and Dr. Sayer.

"Thank you for coming in," the doctor said.

She lifted her eyes from the floor. "I'm Greta."

Harrison, Barbara, and Stan responded in AA unison: "Hi, Greta."

They went around the room, introducing themselves again. When it was Martin's turn, he could barely speak. He seemed unwilling to look at the new girl.

Stan said, "Have *you* ever heard of the Weavers?"

Greta moved her head a fraction. Nope.

"Jesus Christ," Stan said.

The next hour was filled with the polite conversation of people tiptoeing around each other. Martin had stopped talking, Greta had never started, and Stan wouldn't stop. Harrison was entertaining fantasies about turning down his oxygen supply.

Jan said, "We're almost out of time. I'm wondering if people want to share their impressions. How's it going for you? What do you think of the others?"

The others? Harrison wasn't about to touch that one. Jan had said that they were all trauma survivors, with similar experiences. If they'd gone through a fraction of the shit that Harrison had, that had to be Very Special Trauma indeed. It was pretty obvious why Stan was here; he was an old-school victim who'd never gotten tired of showing off his stumps. Barbara had said little about what had happened to her, only that she'd been attacked, and she'd been seeing Dr. Sayer since the '90s. She seemed to have come to terms with it. She was calm, soothing, a natural nurse. Greta, however, was in no shape to help anyone. She was shell-shocked, probably less than a year from whatever supernatural shit went down. And the black kid with the glasses—Martin— Harrison had no idea what to make of him.

And how about the good doctor? He'd only had two sessions with her, after she'd contacted him about joining the group. She'd said she believed his story, which made him think she was lying. *He* wouldn't believe his story.

"I think it's going about like I expected," Harrison said. Meaning: nowhere.

Barbara said, "I was wondering about Martin. He never seems to look at Greta."

"Who can tell?" Stan asked. "He's wearing those damn shades."

"You do seem to be hiding behind them," Barbara said gently to the young man. "I'd like to know what you're thinking, but I can't tell."

Harrison suddenly realized what was going on with the glasses. He leaned forward. "Hey. Martin." The boy didn't move. "*Martin.*"

Martin hesitated, then swiveled his bug-eyed face in Harrison's direction.

Harrison said, "Are you recording this?"

Martin sucked in his lip but did not turn away.

Harrison said, "You're wearing some new kind of Google glasses."

"It's singular," Martin said.

"What?"

"Google *Glass,*" Martin said. "And no, these aren't them. They're actually made by a startup company called—"

"Take them the fuck off."

That *fuck* went off like a little bomb. They'd been so polite so far.

Martin didn't move. No one spoke for a long moment, and then Stan said, "What is he talking about? *Who's* recording this?"

"I'm not recording anything," Martin said.

Harrison had put his hands on his knees, shifting his weight. Everyone in the circle tensed. Greta, next to Harrison, made a small sound too quiet for anyone but him to hear. Dr. Sayer watched him, but made no move to stop him.

Harrison was annoyed. *What?* Leaning forward was not an act of violence. It signified, if anything, the mere willingness to take action. Or perhaps the first move in a sequence: one, Harrison jumping to his feet; two, reaching for doughy, defenseless Martin; three, ripping the glasses from his fucking face.

Harrison leaned back, closed his eyes, and breathed deep. "I would *appreciate* it if you took off the glasses, Martin."

No one spoke. Harrison finally opened his eyes.

Martin was gazing at the floor now. "Dr. Sayer said I could leave them on," he said in a small voice.

Barbara frowned. "Is that true, Jan?"

"I said that he didn't have to take them off to attend the group," Jan said. "He promised me he would not make any recordings, or share what happens here— the same agreement I made with all of you."

"I gave my word," Martin said.

"And I took him at his word," Jan said. "However, I did tell him that the group might want to discuss his wearing of them."

"I don't want a camera in here," Stan said.

Martin made no move to remove the glasses.

Jan said, "Greta, do you have some thoughts on this?"

Harrison watched her without making it obvious that he was watching. She was not a *beautiful* girl—there was something slightly asymmetrical about her features—but she was striking.

"It doesn't matter to me," she said.

"Martin," Jan said. "How are you feeling about this feedback?"

"I don't appreciate the hostility," Martin said. "What about Stan and his mask? Are you going to ask him to get rid of his wheelchair?"

"What does that have to do with anything?" Stan said.

Barbara said, "Do you feel like you *need* the glasses?"

Stan made a derisive sound in the back of his throat.

"I don't appreciate the bullying," Martin said. "From him."

"Me?" Harrison said.

Barbara smiled thinly at him. "You do seem a bit angry."

"I'm not angry." Everyone was looking at him, even Greta. "I'm not!" he said. What the fuck had happened? They were just talking about Martin's glasses, and now they were turning on *him*. "Is this about the swearing? I apologize for that."

"It's not about the swearing," Barbara said. "You seem annoyed that you're in here. With us crazy people."

"That's not accurate," Harrison said. "Jan says we've all experienced trauma. I'll take her at her word."

"You don't have to take her word," Stan said. "Not about me."

"What's yours, then?" Martin said to Harrison. "Your trauma. You haven't said."

"He's Jameson Squared," Greta said.

Shit, Harrison thought. A fan.

"Who?" Stan asked.

"Jameson Jameson," she said. "From the kids' books. The boy who kills monsters."

Barbara looked surprised. She'd heard of him. Martin was more stunned. "I thought those were fiction," he said.

"They are," Harrison said.

Greta said, "Except they're based on a real kid who survived Dunnsmouth. Harrison Harrison."

They stared at him.

"*Fiction*," he said. "Completely made up." Then: "Almost entirely."

Greta was the first to flee the room when the time was up. Harrison followed her, but by the time he got outside she was gone, into the night. She couldn't have gone far, he thought.

The transit van was waiting for Stan. The loading door hung open, and the young driver was working the controls to bring the lift down. The man glanced up as Harrison approached, and Harrison gave him the bro nod again. The driver turned back to the controls.

Harrison walked toward his car, then stopped and turned back. "Excuse me," he said.

The driver looked over his shoulder.

"I gave you the bro nod," Harrison said.

"The what?" The lift clunked down, and the driver stepped back from the lever.

"Twice now," Harrison said. "You're supposed to nod back."

"What the hell are you talking about?" the kid asked.

"The rules," Harrison said. "Cowboys tip their hats at each other. Detectives tap their fedoras. But since we're hatless these days, all we've got is the nod, and returning it isn't optional."

"Are you—?"

"Say 'crazy' and I will beat you to death with Stan's wheelchair."

The kid blanched.

"I'm kidding." Harrison showed his teeth. "You've got four inches and a hundred pounds on me, nobody's that crazy. Now let's practice. Ready?"

Harrison demonstrated. "Tilt the head back, keeping eye contact, but not in a challenging way. Then back level. See? Now you."

The kid stared at him. Then his head tipped back, ever so slightly.

"We'll work on it," Harrison said. He clapped the driver on the shoulder, making him flinch. "But I think we've made excellent progress."

He noticed Martin standing in the light by the house door. He'd been watching the whole exchange through his black glasses, perhaps even recording it, despite what he'd promised the doctor. Harrison threw him a bro nod, and Martin nodded back.

"See?" Harrison said. "Martin gets it." He started for his car and turned again to the driver. "One more thing. Use the fucking access ramp. It's right over there."

He walked to his leased car—he still could not recall what color it was without concentrating—and had just put the key into the ignition when a face appeared at the window. He startled, then laughed to himself.

It was Greta.

He turned the key to get power, and pushed the button to lower the window.

"Were you really there in Dunnsmouth?"

"It was a long time ago," he said.

"Ten years," she said. "That's not so long." She looked to the side. She made no move to leave.

He didn't know what to do with his hands. Starting the car would be rude. Sometimes with crazy people you just had to wait.

After a time she said, "Are you coming back? Next week?"

He hadn't decided yet. The meeting had gone better than he thought it would. They'd already found out his not-so-secret identity, and here he was, still breathing. "I suppose so," he said. "Yeah."

She nodded. She seemed relieved.

He said, "Do you need a ride or something?"

She said, "Do you still kill monsters, Harrison Squared?"

"Look, I don't know what you've read—"

"Yes or no?"

"Sorry," he said. "I don't do that anymore."

"Too bad." She stepped back from the car, then turned and strode across the street. In a moment he lost her in the dark.

Yep, he thought. Definitely the craziest of us.

The rest of us were not so sure. By the time of the last meeting, five months later, we would still not be able to decide, even though there were fewer of us remaining to compete for the title.

Chapter 2

We all returned for the second meeting. And the third.

Barbara was especially grateful that Greta kept coming back. The girl wore the same flesh-covering uniform for each meeting, black on black on black, her thumbs poking through holes in the cuffs of the long T-shirt like lynchpins to hold the armor in place. Barbara felt a twinge of sadness every time she saw the girl check to see if her wrists were exposed.

Greta rarely spoke—but hardly needed to. Stan dominated the discussion in those first meetings, turning each conversational point back to his own distress over being a freak, an outcast. Barbara suspected that the rest of the group was relieved to let the focus stay on him. Harrison didn't have to be challenged on his anger, and Martin didn't have to defend his continued use of the glasses; the young man still could not look in Greta's direction.

Jan didn't bring up any of these issues, and seemed to be willing to let Stan talk and talk. He was weaving his way backward through this story, starting from his current circumstances (terrible), through his life as famous victim (frightening, then tedious, then depressing), arriving after many digressions at the event that made him "the freak he was today." Stan's words. Stan was made of words.

"By then all my friends were dead," Stan said. "Johnny, Davey, Alison, everyone dead except for me and Laura. Dragged off one by one to the smokehouse. A week later they'd be carried back into the barn, their bodies wrapped in burlap, bound by bailing wire. Like sausages. Like mummies. They hung them in the nets next to us.

"Laura was in bad shape. Feverish, hallucinating. I think she'd forgotten where she was. That was a good thing, yes? She didn't know who was hung up beside her."

Stan's tears had started again. Barbara patted his arm. She knew the man was in pain. But who in the room wasn't?

"It was the boy who kept us alive," Stan said. "The youngest of the Weavers, seven, maybe eight years old. They called him Pest. He'd scamper up and down the nets easy as you please, half naked, just a pair of raggedy shorts, wiry as a monkey. He'd bring us water, push bits of food into our mouths. Hose down the ropes when we pissed or shit ourselves. He liked to climb up next to us and jabber in some kinda pidgin English." Stan smiled and shook his head. "I could barely understand what he was saying. He would stroke Laura's hair and coo to her. Most nights he would sleep with us, settle into the nets with his arms and legs in between the loops so he could hang there with us, his own vertical hammock. The older Weavers would beat on him sometimes, but I think they had a soft spot for him too. Or maybe they liked that he kept us alive. Maybe that was his job.

"He tried to help us on harvest days. That dinner bell would ring and the brothers would pull one of us down off the ropes and put us on the table. We'd be thrashing and screaming as they tied off above the cut. It wasn't just Laura who cried and begged, I'm not afraid to admit it. But the Pest—the more we screamed the more he'd whisper and jabber in our ears, trying to soothe us. I remember one harvest— this was so sweet of him—he tried to cover my eyes as they took my left arm. I was so worked up I tried to bite him. I *did* bite him. Drew blood, too. Oh the Weavers laughed at that, made fun of Pest for get- ting careless. But he came back to me and pressed his palms over my eyes again. I felt so bad, losing control like that, but he didn't hold it against me. Not one bit."

Barbara looked around the room. Greta was staring at her hands. Martin was unreadable as ever behind his glasses. Harrison, however, was frowning at Jan.

The doctor was upset. She was sitting very still, but her eyes gleamed from unshed tears. Not for the first time Barbara wondered why any normal person would choose to listen to these stories day after day. Who would make this their job? And why was Harrison looking so disapproving over the doctor showing emotion?

"I only saw the boy cry once," Stan said. "The day they came that last time for Laura. She was in a bad way—the infection was probably in her bloodstream by then, and there wasn't much left of her. I knew what happened next, seen it with the others. Off to the smokehouse. To see *her*."

Stan stopped talking. It was such a surprise that even Greta looked up.

Martin said, "Who?"

Harrison moved his head, a tiny gesture of disappointment. The message was clear: They'd almost gotten someone else to speak! Barbara suppressed a smile, and immediately she felt guilty.

But Stan, surprisingly, did not take the bait. He lifted the oxygen mask to his face and breathed deep. The group waited.

"I don't know what happened to the boy," Stan said

finally. "When they rescued me, they killed the older Weavers—I saw two of the brothers die in front of me—and they killed the thing in the smokehouse. But nobody would talk about a child. They kept all mention of the kid out of the trial, probably to protect him. I used to think about him finding a foster home. Getting adopted. Growing up with real parents . . ."

Stan looked up. "I was glad that they never mentioned the child. Never said a name. Once you get branded a freak . . . that hangs on you."

"Is that what you feel like?" Jan asked. She'd recovered her composure, and her voice was steady. "A freak?"

"Of course," Stan said. "No one can look at me without recoiling."

Jan asked, "Is there anyone in the room that you think is recoiling now?"

Stan glanced at Greta.

"You know, it's not so uncommon to see amputees, since Iraq," Martin said. "Plus you're old."

"What does that have to do with it?" Stan asked.

"I'm just saying. In the seventies or whatever, you were probably more shocking." Martin shrugged. "Now you just look like a diabetic."

"I was in the mall last week," Stan said. "A child looked at me and screamed."

"Really?" Harrison asked. "Screamed?"

Stan looked offended that he could be doubted. "The mother pulled him away from me. And everyone around us noticed what was going on, and then . . ."

And then and then and then. The words rolled out of him.

Barbara listened, but not patiently, as Stan detailed the other times he'd been humiliated or embarrassed in public. He seemed to have catalogued every frown of disgust, every averted gaze. And now no one in the circle would look at him, but not for the reasons he supposed.

When he paused to take a breath from his mask, Barbara said, "We all have scars, Stan." Across the circle from her, Greta toyed with the hole in her sleeve. "Some aren't as on display."

"Amen to that," Harrison said.

"None of you understand," Stan said. "I spend every day in a chair waving *stumps*—"

Barbara stood and Stan abruptly shut up. She hadn't planned on standing. When she realized what she was going to do next, she almost sank back into her seat. The group's eyes were on her.

Greta's eyes were on her.

Barbara took a breath, and then removed her black jacket. She folded it over the chair back and stood for a moment, looking at no one. She was wearing a linen long-sleeved shirt. She owned nothing but long-sleeved shirts.

"Does anyone know what scrimshaw is?" she asked.

"Fuck," Harrison said.

She looked over at him and smiled shyly. She unbuttoned a cuff and began rolling back the sleeve.

"Etchings on whale bone," Stan said. "Old-timey sailor stuff."

"A person who creates scrimshaw is called a scrimshander," Barbara said. "But *the* Scrimshander . . . he doesn't work on whale bones."

She pushed the sleeve up to her bicep. A long, puckered scar ran from the inside of her elbow up past where the sleeve covered it.

"You're from Dunnsmouth?" Harrison asked.

"I visited there," she said. "Just once. I was nineteen." But she wasn't interested in telling her story right now. Stan had already exhausted them, and there'd be plenty of opportunities later. This was for Greta.

Barbara revealed a matching scar on her upper arm. Then she sat down and pulled up her skirt a few inches. Two other scars, starting at each knee. The Scrimshander had made five incisions in all, peeling back her skin to get at large bones. The largest scar was at her sternum, but she decided she'd made her point.

She looked around the room. "So."

The group stared at her. The silence was unbearable.

Harrison grunted. The attention of the group swung to him. He stood up, tugged at his shirt, and lifted it to expose the ribs on his right side. An old, jagged scar puckered the skin. "The Scrimshander's knife got me here," he said. He unbuttoned the top buttons of his shirt and pulled open the collar to show them three round welts, each as big as a half dollar, that looked like old burns. "These were from the suckers of a monster called the Abysmal. And then there's my first one . . ."

He sat and tugged up his right pants leg. The plastic leg started a few inches below his knee. "See, Stan? You're not the only one."

Dr. Sayer put up a hand. "None of you should feel any pressure about sharing before you're ready. This is not a competition."

Stan had already lifted his arm to his mouth. He pulled off the sock with his teeth and let it drop to his lap. The end of the arm looked like a rotted peach. "You can still see the line where the bailing wire cut into the skin—right above the cut."

Barbara watched Greta. Her face had gone pale, and her eyes were fixed on the middle distance. Mentally she'd already fled the room.

I've made a mistake, Barbara thought. Instead of helping the girl, she'd swung the spotlight toward her.

Greta pushed up her sleeve.

Barbara's first impression was of twine: white string that had been wound around her pale arm, arranged into swirls and blocky mazes and jagged bolts. These were not the pale, old scars of Barbara's skin, or Stan's gnarly keloids. The scars were precise markings, intricate as circuit boards, dense as text. They clearly continued up her arm.

"Okay," Stan said to Greta. "You win."

After the meeting, the image of Greta's scars would not leave Barbara's mind. She drove home picturing them, imagining the unseen territory of her skin beneath those dark clothes, guessing at how much of it must be covered with those ridges and swirls. Greta didn't say who had inscribed them on her, or for what purpose, or at what age it had started. Barbara was heartsick at the idea of the girl being subjected to branding. She knew from personal experience the risk of infection, the pain of healing.

But the shapes were so beautiful. And they'd been carved with such artistry.

Her husband's car was already in the garage; they were home from soccer practice then. Usually she would have had supper on the table by now, but on group meeting nights that was impossible. She found Stephen and the boys not in the kitchen but in the living room, a pizza box open on the coffee table.

The three were sitting side by side on the couch, eyes locked on whatever shiny loudness emanated from the TV. Ten-year-old Ryan, shirt off and already tan after a week of sun. Toby, two years younger, still wearing his shin guards and cleats.

"Hey hon," Stephen said without looking up. The boys didn't seem to notice her at all.

She'd known for some time that her husband and sons didn't need her. Oh, perhaps they loved her, but *need*? They would miss the lunches she packed, the appointments she scheduled, the forms she signed. She kept the calendar and sent out the dry cleaning, tracked the boys' ever-changing shoe sizes, cut up the carrots and refilled the water bottles, combed the denim-blue lint from the dryer trap. But these were maintenance activities, easily outsourced. For everything essential, the males of the house had each other. They were a unit, a wolf pack.

She was not sad about this; just the opposite. She'd spent the past few years engineering their independence. They leaned against each other now like three poles. A fourth could only destabilize them.

She made herself a salad and ate it at the breakfast nook. She did not eat alone; the dark outside and the bright kitchen lights made a three-sided mirror of the bay windows so that she was surrounded by Barbaras. She stared at the twin doors of the hall closet, and the seam of light between them from the closet light that one of the boys had left on. She thought about Greta pushing up her sleeve; Harrison, their angry young man, lifting his shirt. She wondered what they thought of *her* scars. Did they understand what they represented, what they hid?

Stephen came into the kitchen and refilled his glass from the Brita pitcher.

"Oh, you had your therapy thing today. How did it go?"

"It was good. Interesting."

"Yeah?" His politeness was reflexive. Kindness was baked into Stephen on the cellular level. "Any break-throughs?"

The boys burst into laughter at something on the TV. His head turned automatically.

"Go finish," she said.

Once Stephen had been her rescuer. He'd seen the girl in the wheelchair parked at the end of the row—the lecture class, on art history, was held in an auditorium—and dared to flirt with her. They were fellow artists, yes? Kindred souls? When she graduated to a cane, he'd asked her to dance. When she threw away the cane, he asked her to marry him. She turned him down. She said, only half joking, that he would leave her if she didn't progress beyond canes to decathlons.

But Stephen was the man who stayed. When she told him she'd lied about the car accident, he did not blink. When she told him some of the things the Scrimshander had done to her (no one knew the whole story), he did not run.

For fifteen years, they were content. He stopped painting but discovered a talent for data analysis, making other kinds of pictures from vast streams of data. There was no financial need for her to work, though she did, taking a series of uninspiring jobs. Finally he said, Why don't you just paint? He knew she needed it, just as he knew, and accepted, her need for privacy, for multiple locks on the door, for sleeping with the bathroom light on. He never asked her why she couldn't say "I love you." They made a life. Sometimes an entire day went by when she didn't think of the Scrimshander.

Then, in their late thirties, a surprise. Not an unwanted pregnancy, but an unwanted desire for a child that appeared without warning and took up residence in her body. She felt ridiculous, as if she were reneging on a contract she'd made with Stephen. But when she finally admitted it to him— "Stephen, I have some news"—he responded with an enthusiasm that frightened her. Had this desire for fatherhood always been in him, but hidden from her because of her craziness? Or was it possible that they could both be so unknown to themselves?

They pursued pregnancy with scientific rigor and religious fervor. They read *What to Expect When*

You're Expecting until they were sick with fear. It was the worst kind of horror story, a child endangered on every page, but they absorbed the moral in every chapter.

And it worked. The babies were born with a minimum of drugs and drama. The infants escaped SIDS and survived croup. The adults weathered sleep dep and stress. They were determined to become what Stephen called The World's Greatest Parenting Team, Non-Asian Division.

When the show ended and the pizza was consumed, Barbara and Stephen expertly separated and funneled the boys into phase 1 of the nighttime routine: homework, dishes, tomorrow's lunches, the charging of devices. They did not have to speak. An hour and a half later, her husband was shooing the boys upstairs to showers and bed. He stopped at the turn of the stairs.

"You're going out?" he asked. He did not add, *again?* Good, polite Stephen.

"I need to get some work done," she said. "I'll be back before breakfast, don't worry."

He started to say something, then changed his mind. A long time ago he'd stopped asking what she was working on, whether it was a new piece or something she'd been painting for weeks. He'd stopped asking when she would show them to him.

"Drive safe," he said.

Drive safe, dress safe, live safe. Retreat to the safest place of all.

She opened the two locks on the apartment door, slipped inside, and immediately flipped the light switch. She stood there for a moment, breathing in the familiar tang of paint thinner, reassuring herself that she was alone.

Every inch of the apartment was visible from this spot at the front door. The main room was just over fifteen feet square with a tiny kitchenette set into the corner. The bathroom was open to her left; she'd removed the door and set it across two metal filing cabinets, making a work table. There were only a few other pieces of furniture: a pair of floor lamps, a wooden easel, a metal folding chair, and a futon with its blue mattress opened flat. A long, wood-framed mirror leaned in the corner. Nothing was wide or high enough to hide an intruder.

The pair of skinny windows at the end of the room were draped, but behind them were sturdy bars. She could feel that the windows had not been opened; the air was as warm and still as when she'd left. She twisted the locks shut behind her, then clacked home the deadbolt like a horizontal exclamation mark.

Safe.

A half-dozen canvases leaned against the walls,

stretched and primed. They'd been waiting for months. On the easel was the work in progress, if one could say that an ongoing failure could progress. She walked past it without looking at it. She drew aside the drapes of one window, then pushed it up a few inches, allowing a feeble draft of cool air. She was on the second floor, so there was little chance someone could see through the window.

The painting on the easel waited for her. She sat on the futon and looked up at it. As she'd done many times before, she'd painted a set of double doors, pale as her skin, and a seam between them glowing with golden light.

I left you a message.

She had not touched the canvas in weeks. There was nothing wrong *with* the painting, except that it was the wrong painting entirely. The doors should be open, revealing . . . something. A person, an object, a promised land. Or perhaps an abstract design, too difficult to translate into words. She would know it when she saw it, but she could not paint it until she saw it. Every time she'd attempted to force her way past those doors—and she'd tried a dozen times—she created a lie. An offense. The results were good only for burning.

She stood and removed her jacket, then blouse and skirt and underwear, and set them on the bed. How scandalized would Dr. Sayer have been if she'd gone this far during the meeting? She might have stopped Stan's heart.

She went into the bathroom. The apartment's open layout and clear sightlines were requirements, but what decided her on this place was the giant prewar bathtub. It was a cast-iron clawfoot tub, high-backed and swooping, that took up most of the narrow bathroom like a plump aristocrat. The porcelain interior shone like cold milk.

She turned the taps (which were not the original hardware, but stubby, characterless replacements), and waited while the water warmed. She was and was not thinking about the mirror. Months ago she'd driven screws into the bathroom wall and strung long loops of hanging wire. She'd hung the big frame there, then, embarrassed, took it down, even though no one ever came into the apartment.

After a long moment she went into the other room and brought back the mirror. It did not feel like a decision. It was something her body was doing, an action she was merely failing to veto. Perhaps, she thought—in the part of her brain that was noticing what was happening—this is the absence the recovering alcoholic feels as the glass fills. The blankness of the compulsive gambler as the next twenty slides into the slot machine.

She attached the mirror to the wall. The top wire was much longer than the bottom, so that the mirror leaned out across the tub. She got into the water, concentrating to make her nerve-damaged limbs move correctly, and when she looked up it was at a second tub, a second Barbara, suspended from above. The woman's skin gleamed, and the scars were like silver trails.

The Scrimshander first made a filet of her limbs. He peeled back the skin of her arms to get at each humerus, keeping her half-sedated with strong alcohol as he worked. He moved carefully around the major arteries, preventing her from bleeding out. Over the course of a day and night he moved on to each femur, then finally the long crease at her sternum. He told her she had beautiful bones, and that he had made her even more beautiful.

I left you a message.

She never got to see what he had drawn. The police found her, unconscious, and by the time she awoke the doctors had stitched her closed.

Greta was so lucky, Barbara thought. What had been done to her was right there, written where anyone could see.

Chapter 3

We were all surprised every time Stan made it to another meeting. If he wasn't yet knocking at death's door, he seemed to be rolling up the access ramp to it, huffing into his mask, hauling his collection of failing organs with him. After several months we were all deeply knowledgeable about his ailments and injuries, his medicines and their side effects, his ongoing battle with incompetent doctors and heartless nurses and corrupt insurance clerks. The medical industrial complex, he said, was a God damn mess, and it was a miracle he was still kicking.

And yet, not only did he make it to the Elms every week, he arrived early.

Stan bragged to the group how he'd lied to the van service, told them the meeting was a half hour earlier than it was. The same smart-ass kid picked him up every week. Knocked on the door, wouldn't use the bell, walked right in if Stan didn't get there fast enough. The kid would stand there making faces behind that God damn lumberjack beard, wrinkling his nose at the house that Stan had spent four decades in. "How the hell can a man with no hands be a hoarder?" the kid said once. He'd shove stuff out of the way, kicking Stan's belongings like they were garbage, or worse, picking them up like he was appraising their value.

"Why do you have a pistol?" the kid asked. It was a .357 police swing-out revolver, brand new and still in its case. Stan had found it on eBay.

"None of your damn business," Stan said. There was a lot more than the .357 in the house, but the kid didn't need to know that.

"How do you fire it?"

"Shut up," Stan said. "We're late."

Somewhere in the house were his prosthetics. He'd gone through a dozen of them before giving up on them twenty years ago. They weren't anything like the high-tech robot parts the soldiers had now; these were old-fashioned hooks and flesh-toned mannequin hands and strap-on shoes—original pirate material. Uncomfortable as hell.

These days he rented hands, day nurses, and Merry Maids and Meals-on-Wheels volunteers. The new ones always suggested he move into assisted living. They didn't suggest it twice. *I survived on scraps!* he told them. *For months! You think you can put me in a God damn prison?*

Oh, he could still crank up a good rant. The young ones quit the first time he reduced them to tears, and good riddance. He couldn't stand wimps. He could instantly spot every variety of bad egg: the thief, the layabout, the cell phone watcher, the idiot. It usually didn't take more than a phone call to get them transferred, and if that failed he could get them to quit soon enough. They thought he was old and helpless.

He could see it in the eyes of the group, too. Well, most of their eyes. The youngest one, Martin, still wouldn't take off the sunglasses. He decided to bring it up with Dr. Sayer before the meeting started.

As the eldest member of the group, he thought it a good idea to confer with the doctor before the meetings and share thoughts about how therapy was going. Often she came downstairs right as the meeting was scheduled to start, leaving them no time to talk, but some weeks he could get a couple of minutes of one-on-one time with her.

Today he was lucky. He'd commanded the driver to wait with him outside the conference room, and Dr. Sayer came down the stairs a few minutes before six.

Her smile was bright and unforced. "Early again, Stan?"

The first time he'd met her, at the pre-group interview, that smile had struck a chime in his heart. It was not lust (though he was not above those feelings, despite lacking the ability to act on them), but something finer, almost familial. In another life she could have been his daughter. Her wide green eyes were steady and accepting. She always looked at him directly, without revulsion. Seeing all of him.

"Early is on time," Stan said. Before she could walk into the room, he asked her about Martin's glasses. Did she realize that no one had mentioned them since the first meeting? It had been weeks and weeks. "Everyone's so nervous about conflict they don't want to bring 'em up again," he said.

"That's a perceptive insight," Dr. Sayer said. Stan felt the warmth of her approval. True, it was Barbara who'd suggested to him that conflict avoidance was a reason for the silence, but Stan had been thinking much the same thing, so it was his idea too.

"I think you should bring that up in group," the doctor said.

"Martin will just say that you let him keep the glasses on," Stan said. Which is what Stan had told Barbara.

"Maybe," the doctor said. "But that's something we can talk about, too."

That was her thing: Everything had to happen in the group. And maybe he *should* share this insight.

"I'll think about it," Stan said. He waved an arm to get the driver's attention. "Wheel me."

The kid didn't move.

"Please take me into the room," Stan said evenly.

The kid sighed. Stan knew he was rolling his eyes, trying to look like a big man in front of the doctor. Well, to hell with you, kid.

Stan directed the driver to his regular spot, between the chairs that Harrison and Barbara always went to. He liked Barbara almost as much as he did Dr. Sayer. He was so happy the woman had sat beside him on the first day, and happier still that they'd stuck to their seats as if they'd been assigned. Dr. Sayer, thank God, had not inflicted any teambuilding exercise on them and forced them to shuffle their positions.

Barbara arrived a few minutes later. Stan lowered his mask and said hello. She smelled like a proper woman; just a touch of expensive perfume, nothing cloying. He liked to breathe her in. Sometimes, if he shared something awful or sad, she'd pat his arm. Dr. Sayer, despite her obvious affection for him, never touched him.

"How are you doing, Stan?" Barbara asked warmly.

"Oh, can't complain," he said. He told her about his eye doctor, who wanted to do cataract surgery on him. His vision wasn't as good as it used to be, but he wasn't blind, not yet. "A dozen other things will kill me before I need to fix my eyes," he said. Martin and Harrison came into the room. "I don't need any more people coming at me with scalpels."

"I think they use lasers now," Harrison said. He was dressed in a suit jacket and T-shirt, which Stan thought was a ridiculous combination. Make up your damn mind; either wear the whole suit with a man's shirt and tie, or go play basketball.

"Just another kind of knife," Stan said.

"Lightsaber," Martin said.

Greta took her seat next to Harrison. Stan had never gotten close enough to Greta to sniff her, but he wouldn't be surprised if she wore men's deodorant. She was almost certainly homeless, or a lesbian, or a homeless lesbian. Definitely didn't like men. Every week she sat across the circle from him, glowering. Hardly ever spoke. What the hell was she doing here, if she wasn't even going to talk? Also, he was pretty sure she wasn't wearing a bra.

"Who'd like to start?" Dr. Sayer asked.

No one said anything. Dr. Sayer turned her eyes to Stan.

He lifted his eyes from Greta's chest. What was the doctor wanting? Oh right. "I want to talk about the glasses again," Stan said.

Martin looked up, wary.

"No one's asking you to take them off," Barbara said to Martin. Then to Stan: "Are you, Stan?"

"No." But he thought, Not yet.

"Good," Martin said. "Because I'm not."

"I'm not telling you to," Stan said.

"Here's what I want to know," Harrison said. "If you're not recording anything right now—"

"I'm not," Martin said.

"Then why can't you take them off, just for this meeting?"

Stan was annoyed that Harrison had stolen his thunder. "Yeah," Stan said. "Why?"

Martin mumbled something.

"What was that?" Stan asked.

"I *said*, I can't turn off the game."

Before anyone else could jump in, Stan asked the obvious question: "What the hell are you talking about?"

"It's called *Deadtown*," Martin said. "It's an augmented reality RPG."

Stan said, "Augmented . . ."

"It's a video game," Martin said. "But you play it in the real world. The game turns people on the street into zombies, and you actually *see* their faces transformed through the camera. The filters are wicked cool, completely dynamic."

Stan still had no idea what he was talking about. But it was certainly the most animated Martin had ever been in group.

"You get points by killing the zombies," Martin said. "You can pick up weapons that the game world drops for you, or buy them online. You just make your hand into a gun shape, and—" The fingers of his right hand curled. "There. A pistol." He made another shape. "Or a knife. Or a sword."

"You walk around pointing your *finger* at people?" Stan said.

"It's not that easy," Martin said. "You have to shoot them in the head to kill them. Or get close enough to chop their heads off." He made a flicking gesture with his hand. "If they touch you, they turn *you* into a zombie."

"You do this in public," Stan said disbelievingly.

"Nobody knows what I'm doing," Martin said. "I played for months and nobody noticed. And they don't know they're zombies. I just—" He pointed his hand. "Bang. *Splat.* The sound effects are awesome. The glasses use bone conduction speakers, so you actually feel the back blast."

"That's . . . awful," Barbara said.

"The entire sound design's incredible. Sirens in the distance, people screaming, *gun*shots. The game could actually get you to *duck*. Totally insane. And the gameplay. You don't level up like in other games, you don't get more hit points or better weapons. It just gets more and more intense. The apocalypse keeps snowballing. I mean, I kept playing, and more and more zombies appeared on the streets. Even the buildings started to change. Like, *crumbling*. Cars burning, corpses on the sidewalk. I'd walk into the 7-Eleven and there'd be a headless corpse slumped against the beverage cooler. The guy at the register would have bullet wounds in his face.

"And the zombies kept coming. Some days—some days the streets were filled with the dead. Gray faces on everybody. *Way* too dangerous to leave my apartment. I'd snipe from my window, or go down to the front door and try to clear a path . . . but sometimes there were too many of them. Impossible. Some days I'd have to wait for hours for a lull, just so I could get to work."

Stan said, "Why didn't you just stop?"

Martin shook his head at the stupidity of the question. "There's no—how do I explain this? There's no break, no pause between levels. You don't even have to save progress. They've removed all *reasons* for stopping. You can go all day, all night."

"Until you starve to death," Harrison said.

"So what?" Stan asked. "Just take off the damn glasses. Why is that so hard?"

"You don't know what it's like," Martin said. "To be immersed like that." He looked up. "Every other game, there's this *wall*. The screen that keeps you out, and you can't get to the other side, no matter how hard you try. But this—I was *inside*. All the time. And it was amazing."

Martin looked down at his hands. Or rather, the eyeglasses were aimed at his hands.

"And then I started seeing things."

"Right," Harrison said. "*Then* you started seeing things."

"No. Things that weren't supposed to be in the game." Martin shook his head. "It wasn't just the standard monsters anymore. I saw this thing. It wasn't a zombie, it was . . . I don't know. White, slippery skin. Too many arms, too many fingers. Like a lizard, but . . . weirder."

"Ah," Harrison said knowingly. Which annoyed Stan immensely. *Ah* what?

"I could barely look at it," Martin said. "It wasn't just one thing. Well, it was one thing, but overlaid on itself. All lizards."

"Like seeing it from all angles at once," Greta said.

Martin looked up. "Yes! Like that! But not just space—like I was seeing it over time."

"*Nude Descending a Staircase,*" Dr. Sayer said.

"What?" Stan asked.

"It's a painting by Duchamp," Barbara said.

"Why don't you Google it?" Harrison asked Martin. "We'll wait."

"I know what she's talking about," Martin said. "These things are like the woman in the painting, but . . . worse. They move. I get nauseous looking at them. And the people have no idea that these things are right next to them. But I could see them. They left after-images, like trails. *Wakes.* So even when they weren't in front of me, I could tell where they'd been. There were tracks everywhere through the city. We were overrun.

"At first I thought I'd leveled up," Martin said. "But that wasn't it. These things weren't part of the game. I checked the forums—nobody was seeing this. Nobody had heard of anything like this. It didn't make game sense, either. I couldn't do anything to them. I couldn't shoot them, or knife them. They'd just *leer* at me."

"They could see you?" Dr. Sayer asked.

"Oh yeah."

"Did they talk to you?" It was Greta.

"Not to me, but—" He shook his head. He didn't look at her. Hadn't ever looked at the girl since the group began. "They whispered to people on the street. I could hear them, making this sound . . . but it wasn't words. I don't think it was words.

"There was this guy who hung around our block. My roommates called him Dog Man, because he was always sniffing the air. Wrinkling his nose like something stank. Talking to himself. They thought he was schizophrenic, but I could see the thing with him. Speaking to him. And Dog Man was listening. And sometimes it would be whispering to him, and he'd look at me like he *knew* me.

"I stopped going out. It wasn't just Dog Man. The streets were full all the time now. My apartment was the last safe place. At least I thought so." His smile was a surprised twitch.

"I was lying in my bed. It was late, maybe two or three in the morning. The sirens were dying down. A building was on fire across the street, and the flames were flickering in my window, making this weird light in the room. Which is impossible, I know that. Glasses can add pixels, they can't add light, but still, I could see everything in the room, lit up by the fire-light, and everything seemed to be in motion. No, like it was *about* to move. Quivering, like . . . I don't know. Something under pressure, deep under the ocean. I remember looking at my desk, and my shirt was draped across the back of the chair, like a man hunched up in the dark. Waiting. Everything in the room was vibrating, on the edge of bursting open, like a jack-in-the-box. You're turning, turning, and you can feel the lid *trembling*. You can't help yourself, you've got to turn the crank a little more, just daring yourself . . ."

Martin ran a hand through his hair. "At the end of the bed is the door to my closet. It's a heavy wooden thing, not a regular closet door, more like a door to another apartment. Maybe it was, once. The building's old, the apartments are all too small. Anyway, the door sticks all the time. I usually have to yank to get it open. But that night, I'm on my back, looking straight at it. And it starts to open.

"And there was nothing there. My closet was gone. Where it used to be was a tunnel. The walls were rock. Damp, shining, like, I dunno, wet coal. It went back a long ways.

"Then I saw the hand. I yelled and pushed myself backward. It had come up from the floor and grabbed the footboard. It wasn't human, it was one of theirs—gray, webbed, fingertips like knives. Then a second hand came up. And the creature pulled itself onto the bed. Smiling.

"I scrambled off the bed and ran for the door to the hallway. Later I realized the thing must have come out of the tunnel and crawled across the floor, out of my line of sight. Maybe I could have shut the door. But all I was thinking then was that it was in the room with me, and I had to get out.

"So I ran. I grabbed my backpack and bugged out. My roommates were in their bedrooms asleep, but I knew they couldn't help me. Wouldn't help me. I ran into the hallway, downstairs. I'm standing there in the street like a crazy person. And I realized I'd yanked off the frames. I was holding them in my hand, and now the sirens were gone. The fires. For the first time in weeks everything was normal. Everything looked totally normal.

"Even Dog Man.

"He was standing there on the sidewalk looking at me, a weird smile on his face. He was alone. I knew that the lizard thing he'd been talking to, his *partner*, was up there in my room. I started screaming at him. Take it! It's yours! I decided I was never coming back. If the creatures wanted the place, they could have it."

"They can't do that," Harrison said.

The attention of the group turned toward him.

"They can't *take* a place, because they can't cross over."

"And you *know* this," Martin said skeptically.

"They're called dwellers," Harrison said. Greta made a noise and Harrison said, "They're not like the dwellers in the books. They're more vicious. And if they could get you, they would, glasses or not."

"But they can't?" Barbara asked.

"They're not here. What he's seeing—he's peeking through to the other side. That's where they live. They're always there, watching us. Looking for a way to get through."

"You don't understand," Martin said.

"Oh, I think I do," Harrison said. "Nobody knows as much as I do about the dwellers."

"You don't know what they can do!" Martin yelled.

51

The boy was flushed, breathing hard. He might have been crying, but the glasses made it difficult to tell. "They're here, *whispering*."

"Do you see any monsters now?" Barbara asked.

Martin stared at his hands. Finally he nodded.

"Where are they, Martin?"

"There," he said. He lifted his head and nodded at Greta.

"You see a monster next to her?" Dr. Sayer asked.

"No," Martin said. "She *is* the monster."

Chapter 4

We had been so careful with her, in meeting after meeting, because we believed her to be the most vulnerable of us. Her silence we took to be a great wound that could close only with time and our support. So in the first months of the group the rest of us talked and talked, telling our stories, working on our "issues," while we circled around the void that was Greta. We tacitly agreed that we would wait for her. Let her come to trust us. And make no sudden moves.

We didn't realize that by questioning Martin, we would make the most sudden move of all. In the space of a few minutes we outed her. Finally, we thought, we'll hear the story of her scars.

Then she stood up and walked out of the room.

Jan went after her but failed to convince her to come back inside. The meeting ended awkwardly, with all of us retreating into silence. Martin was obviously still angry, but he refused to say anymore.

The next week he was still angry. How could he explain to the others what he saw in Greta? She *burned*, radiating heat. Yet she came into the room and took her seat as usual. Then the meeting started and she sat there as if she were just like them. As if nothing he'd said had mattered.

After ten minutes he could stand it no longer.

"Tell us," Martin said. "Tell us what you are."

Greta said nothing.

"You can't just sit there!" he said.

Jan leaned forward. "Each of us gets to decide how much to reveal, and when," she said. He took that as a veiled reference to what he hadn't shared yet with the group, but that was unfair; what Greta was hiding was so much worse. "That's the only way the group can work."

Greta looked as if she were about to speak, then she shook her head. "I will tell you. I promise. But not now."

"We have seventy-eight minutes," Martin said. The frames' clock glowed in the upper right of his vision.

"It's not about the *time remaining*," Harrison said. His voice was dismissive as always. Martin knew that the man had never liked him. "Take off the glasses. If you're seeing her as a monster, you're not seeing her as a person."

"Wow, that is *so* profound," Martin said.

Barbara said, "Martin, we're not attacking you."

"No, *he* is. Trying to put this back on me." Martin sat down and crossed his arms to steady his hands. "Is *that* the way the group works, Jan?"

Dr. Sayer regarded him with that distant, professional gaze. Watching them from the other side of the glass, analyzing them. Not for the first time Martin wondered why she'd assembled these freaks. Did she *enjoy* making them tell their ghost stories? No normal psychiatrist could *believe* the crazy shit they were telling her, so she was doing something else. Writing a book about them probably. Or collecting evidence for the next new diagnosis for the *DSM*: Supernatural Victim Delusion. She should be paying *them*. (Not that he was totally up to date on his payments. He'd been forced to delay the last couple of checks.)

Martin said to her, "So. Are you going to take a stand here?"

"I'm not sure what you're asking," Jan said.

"It's simple," Martin said. "You're the doctor. You're supposed to do what's best for your patients. So now you have to take a stand. Are you going to protect *us*, or . . . *her*?"

Jan hesitated, and Martin said, "Unless you think I'm making all this up."

Jan shook her head. "I believe you're sincere when you tell us what you see through the glasses. But Greta is also—"

"Let me try 'em on," Stan said. "I'll look."

"Let her finish," Harrison said.

"She *knows* she's a danger," Martin said to the doctor. "So let's stop talking and *do* something." He looked at Harrison. "You're the big monster hunter. You're going to just sit there?"

"Greta is not your problem," Harrison said.

Jan said, "Martin, you saw Greta on the first day. Was she a monster then?"

"Can we please stop using that word?" Barbara said.

"Jesus," Martin said under his breath. Then to Jan he said, "Yes. She was."

"But you didn't leave," Jan said. "Every week you came back. You sat in the room with her, six feet from her. I'm curious about that. Would you like to talk about that?"

He understood now; no one wanted to talk about the truth, with the possible exception of Stan. The old man seemed ready to believe him, but all Barbara wanted was for conflict to go away. Harrison was allied with Greta, trying to get in her pants. And Dr. Sayer would rather make this Martin's problem than deal with the actual fucking monster in the room. It was no different in group than anywhere else.

Martin stood. "If she won't talk," he said sarcastically, "then there's nothing to talk *about.*"

It felt good to be the one to march out this time. When he reached the front door of the building he paused. No one had called out to him. No one was running after him.

Fuck them.

He'd walked a dozen feet down the sidewalk before he realized that he had not scanned for lizards—scratch that—*dwellers.* He stopped, turned. It was near dusk, and there was no one close by, and no otherworldy creatures that he could detect. However, the marks of their passage were everywhere: Streaks of blue-black (streaks that after sundown would change to a pulsing silver in his display; he could control the graphics settings) painted the sidewalks and streets. So many here, way more than in other parts of the city. The Elms, he'd realized on the first day he'd come here, was *interesting* to them. He'd even briefly entertained the idea that this Dr. Sayer must be a *Deadtown* player, but then he met her and no, she'd never seen a pair of frames.

Martin's bus was scheduled to arrive in ten minutes at a stop two blocks away. His CTA app—

which as far as he could tell had not been haunted, spiritualized, or otherwise corrupted by *Deadtown*— told him that the bus was running on time. But still he didn't leave. He walked a little way down the street, where he could watch the front doors of the Elms, and waited.

Harrison and Greta were first out, and they exited together. Martin watched as they walked, heads low in conversation. The air seemed to shimmer in Greta's wake, like heat above a highway. Harrison stopped beside his car, a gleaming BMW coupe that was more expensive than anything Martin could afford. They exchanged a few words. Greta shrugged. Then they continued down the sidewalk.

So, Martin thought. A date.

Jan had not prohibited them from meeting outside the group. She said it usually happened, so why make a rule? She did ask that when members did meet outside that they tell the group about it. Anything that happened to members of the group was fuel for the group's work. Secret alliances, the doctor said, could divide them.

Martin watched them walk away, the air trembling behind them, twisting the light like beach glass. Even after they turned the corner, the effect did not dissipate. He stood there for several minutes, not caring about his bus now, and after ten minutes the warp remained. He wondered how long it would last—hours? Days? What *was* she? She cut through the world like a knife, and the scars she left behind were deeper than any made by the dwellers.

Police tape still crisscrossed the front door of his apartment. He'd wondered if the landlord had changed the locks, and so was relieved to find that his key still worked. And why not? The rent was paid a month in advance. He was not a criminal. Not even a suspect. He pushed open the door, then slipped under the tape. He closed the door quietly behind him.

The living room was dark. He was happy to not see whatever stains marked the carpet.

He had not been close friends with his roommates. The four of them were at most business partners: They'd been brought together by the online Mix-Master of Craigslist to share rent, that was all. In the frames he'd tagged them all as "Dave." The fact that one of them was white and two of them were East Asian made less difference than their tastes in gaming systems. One Dave was a console drone; another liked handhelds and played ancient DS games; the third preferred indie board games with names like *Push Fight* and *Zug un Zug*. Martin was the only one with an experimental bent. Oh they tried on his frames, but one of the Daves got motion-sick from them, and they'd called them "immature tech."

He'd tried to tell them about *Deadtown* but they weren't interested. So, when the other creatures began to invade the game, he kept that information to himself. When he locked himself in his room and didn't talk to them for days, they didn't mind. As long as he paid his share of the rent he could do what he wanted.

And when he ran out of the apartment, and told Dog Man to take what he wanted, he didn't give the Daves a second thought.

Martin did not turn on the lights, though he knew from the glow of charging devices that the power was still on. He did not want to alert the landlord. He made his way back to his bedroom, opened the door, and turned on the flashlight app on his phone.

He slowly exhaled. Dog Man, it seemed, had not entered the room.

He opened his backpack and began to fill it. He stuffed in clothes, his external hard drives, the Sony PSP, the box of Arduino chips. Then he knelt and popped the case of the custom-built PC and yanked the hard drive, motherboard, and graphics card. These last two were the most expensive components, and he hoped he could sell them. There might have been financial support for the victims of crimes, but as it turned out there was no financial support for the crime adjacent. It didn't matter to anyone but himself that he was homeless now. His savings were gone, and his credit—never very good—was maxed out. He'd have to sell everything he could and try to buy back what he needed later. He'd learned that he was afraid of the homeless shelters, and terrified of living in the streets.

He looked around one more time. His backpack was already overflowing, but perhaps, if the landlord didn't find a renter, he could sneak back in again later.

As for tonight . . .

He didn't want to sleep in this place. But he didn't know where else to go. He shut the door, and moved his desk chair so that the chair back was wedged under the knob. He didn't have to be afraid of Dog Man. The man had been arrested while still in the apartment. Hadn't even tried to run. But there were other people out there, people listening to the whispers.

Martin shouldn't have told the dwellers that this was their place now. He shouldn't have invited them in. He lay on his back, watching the room's single window, and hoped that they hadn't noticed that he'd returned.

At the next meeting, Martin sat in his usual spot, waiting. Stan complained about nurses creeping around on the second floor of his house where he didn't go anymore, going through his things, looking for valuables. Then Barbara talked about an apartment where she went at night to do photography or painting or something. These people had houses on top of houses. Harrison probably kept summer homes on each coast.

Greta, once again, sat there saying nothing.

"I know it doesn't make any sense," Barbara was saying. "I know I'd be safer at home with my husband. We have an excellent alarm system. But it's only in the studio that I feel safe."

"Safe from what?" Jan asked.

"The Scrimshander," Barbara said.

"But he's dead," Greta said. She looked at Harrison. "It's in the books. Lub stabbed him through the heart with a harpoon."

Barbara looked shaken. "Is that true?"

"You can't trust what's in the books," Harrison said.

"Amen," Stan said.

"But in this case," Harrison said. "Yes, he's dead. I saw it myself. And it wasn't a harpoon through the heart—that's the kiddie version. We cut off his head and burned it."

"But he's not human," Barbara said. "He *could* come back."

Stan said, "You want him to come back."

"Of course not!" Barbara said.

"Not really come back," the old man said. "But just

to end the waiting. I'm always waiting. Sometimes I think I'm still up there in the nets, the boy running his fingers through my hair, waiting for the Weavers to take me down for the next treatment."

"Stan," Harrison said. "Let Barbara finish."

Barbara was staring straight ahead—in Greta's direction, but Martin thought that she wasn't seeing anyone in the room. "He carved pictures into me," Barbara said. "The last thing he said to me was, 'I left you a message.'" She inhaled shakily and seemed to come to herself. "But if he's dead, who's going to tell me what he drew?"

"How about x-rays?" Harrison asked. "MRIs?"

"X-rays don't show the surface of the bone," Barbara said. "MRIs don't work either. Ultrasound gets close, but it won't show the fine marks."

No one had any more ideas. Greta said nothing— of course.

Then Jan said, "Tell us more about the apartment, Barbara. Why do you think you feel safer there?"

Barbara started talking about some kind of bathtub. Martin watched the clock on his frames, wondering how long it would take them to finally talk about Greta. She glowed in his peripheral vision. He thought he was going to scream. Then he took off his frames.

Barbara stopped talking. He'd jerked in his seat, and the legs had loudly scraped the floor.

63

"I'm sorry," he said. He put the glasses back on.

"What is it?" Jan asked.

When he'd taken off the frames, he'd glanced at Greta, and she was still glowing. He could still see the fire behind her eyes. That should have been impossible.

Jan said, "I've been getting the feeling that you had something to say, Martin. Did you want to say something to Barbara?"

Not to Barbara, he thought. "Please. Go on," he said.

"It's okay," Barbara said. "Say what's on your mind."

That flash of Greta's true nature, without the filter of the software, had thrown him off. It took him a moment to realize that this was the moment to speak he'd been waiting for.

"I feel like we're being judged," Martin said. He'd thought about this sentence for a while. That "we" was strategically placed. This wasn't about him, he was saying; this was about the group being attacked.

"By me?" Jan asked. Her tone made the question sound sincere, not at all defensive.

He nodded in Greta's direction.

"*Me?*" Greta asked.

"You can't come week after week and not talk," Martin said. "You listen to us, but you don't share anything of yourself."

"You're still mad about last week," Harrison said.

Martin started to deny it, then said, "Yes! Yes I am. Everybody's pretending like nothing happened."

"She's not a monster," Harrison said. "Those scars—"

"Then let her prove it," Martin said. "She should share something. Anything. Put some cards on the table."

"I'm right here," Greta said softly. "Please stop talking about me in third person."

Martin still could not look at her directly. The monster burned in her, heat spilling from her mouth and eyes. A basilisk.

"I'd prefer not to," Greta said.

"You can't keep hiding from us," Martin said.

"I won't. I just . . . I can't. Not right now."

"That's what you keep saying." He looked at Harrison. "But you talk to him, don't you?"

"Excuse me?" Harrison said.

Jan said, "Does anyone else have thoughts on Greta's participation in the group?"

No one spoke. The silence dragged.

"Cowards," Martin said.

Harrison and Greta again left the building together. They did not pause at Harrison's car this time, but strolled on down the sidewalk, walking side by side, almost touching shoulders. Intimate.

Martin watched from across the street, but he

did not move until they turned the corner. He did not need to follow closely. He'd tuned the frames to Greta's frequency, and her trail hung in the air, clear as the lightpath of a Tron bike.

He followed the monster's shimmering wake down two blocks, then across a parklet. The pair was far ahead of him. They crossed the street and entered an Irish pub with a wide front window. Harrison held the door for her.

Night was falling, and the streetlamps were humming to life. Martin stepped into a doorway of a closed stationery store that was kitty-corner from the bar window, about thirty feet away. He waited, thinking of stealth games like *Gunpoint* and *Metal Gear Solid*. If only the frames would throw up a red exclamation mark over his head if he was detected.

After a few minutes he was rewarded. Harrison and Greta took a table near the window, lit up as if on screen. They learned toward each other, talking earnestly. There didn't seem to be any other customers in the pub.

Greta burned, and he could barely look at her. He studied Harrison's face instead, trying to squeeze meaning out of every expression. That smile; was he flirting with her? Laughing? Then Harrison hopped up and returned with their drinks. When he sat down again he was facing slightly away from the window.

Martin stepped out of the doorway and moved closer to the bar, staying close to the brick wall of the building. He took up a new position at the mouth of a narrow alley. The couple wouldn't be able to see past their reflection in the window; if he stayed in the shadows, he should be invisible to them. He watched them for ten, fifteen minutes, recording every second for later analysis. Unfortunately there was no app he knew of that could lip-read from video. HAL 9000, already way past due, was still in the future.

Harrison reached across the table and laid his hand on hers. Martin nearly laughed when Greta pulled away.

"Hey," a voice behind him said. "Pervert."

He turned, and a fist caught him in the throat. He went down to his knees, gagging. A boot caught him under the ribs and drove the air out of him. His brain flared in panic. *Dwellers*, he thought. *Finally.*

But no. These weren't the lizards; they were humans in sharp-toed boots and dark clothes, though he couldn't figure out how many of them there were. Two, three? He lifted his head, and something hard smashed into his face. Pain blinded him.

"Don't even *look* at her," a voice said. A woman's voice.

He lay on the sidewalk, trying to curl into a ball. They were kicking him, and there seemed to be dozens of them now, coming from all angles. He could not defend himself. He couldn't breathe. And the frames—oh God, the frames had been torn from his face. He was defenseless.

Then the blows stopped. He tried to speak, but his mouth would not work correctly. Maybe they were finished with him?

He turned his head and saw a dark-haired girl watching them. She was ten or eleven years old, dressed in jeans and a pink cotton jacket. She did not seem scared by what was happening to him. She seemed . . . *interested*. If he'd been wearing the frames, he might have thought she'd been rendered by the game software.

Then his arms were seized, and they dragged him backward across the pavement. He caught a glimpse of faces rendered hawkish by streetlight and shadow. Then they pulled him further into the alley, out of even that light.

They weren't finished with him, he realized. Not at all.

Chapter 5

We were not yet a fully functioning group. Early on, Dr. Sayer had outlined the typical stages—forming, storming, norming, and perhaps, someday, performing—but cautioned us against thinking that these stages were clearly defined, or that progress was going to be linear. There was no ladder. The work of the group was to follow wherever the work of the group led. Sometimes that meant we doubled back to the same issues again and again.

Often it came down to trust. The patients among us did not trust each other, and some of them did not trust the doctor. Did she really believe these outrageous stories? And how, exactly, were they supposed to "get better"? What possible treatment plan could there be for people who'd seen the truth? Because most of all what we didn't trust was the world.

Dr. Sayer understood this, better than the others could know. She knew—*knew*—that the universe was full of malevolent creatures, and that there was no protection from them. All the group members, Jan included, were certain to die, almost certainly alone. What the patients didn't understand was that this was the human condition. The group members' horrific experiences had not exempted them from existential crises, only exaggerated them.

One-on-one therapy was sometimes not the best tool to bring this point home. Jan had been Barbara's personal therapist for three years now, and the woman would not take the news from her. Barbara's torture had, in her mind, transformed her into a separate class of person. She could impersonate the perfect mother, she believed, but never be her. She could *pass*. But no citizen of the normal, she believed, could possibly understand what she'd experienced. What she'd become.

What Barbara needed were peers. Others like her, who also lived close enough to meet with her. Jan knew all about Stan; she had followed his status even before she started her practice, and in some ways, had started it because of him. But she had never approached him. She could reach out to his therapist, but that wasn't enough; two members could not make a group. She needed five at a bare minimum.

Then a psychotherapist in the suburbs, a woman

Jan knew only in passing, called to say, "I've got someone who might be up your alley." Jan had authored a chapter in a book about treating clients who'd experienced extreme trauma: torture victims, witnesses to the murders of loved ones, those who'd murdered loved ones for no reason they understood. She often got referrals for these types of patients.

"PTSD?" Jan asked.

"That's part of it," the other therapist said. "But I meant, uh, the other alley."

Word had also gotten around about Jan's interest in the paranormal, or rather, in patients who blamed the paranormal for their presenting problem, but exhibited no other symptoms of schizophrenia. Sometimes they were *also* torture victims, witnesses to the murder of loved ones, or murderers—and who'd killed for reasons that no one would believe.

No one except Dr. Jan Sayer.

"She told me she murdered over fifty people," the other therapist said. "But that's not what the police report said. There was a fire, and she escaped—the only one to get out alive. At first I figured her problem to be survivor's guilt."

Jan said, "At first?"

"By the end of the session she told me that some kind of angel had killed them—but that she was still responsible."

"An angel," Jan said flatly.

The other therapist laughed. "Or something. So you'll take her?"

"I'll talk to her," Jan said. "She might be right for a small group I've been thinking about."

Speaking the idea aloud seemed to act like a summoning. Within days of that call, Jan received referrals for two more locals, one of them semi-famous, the other a fragile young man whose roommates had been murdered by a homeless man.

She had her five.

Then, after she got them into the same room, she wondered what the hell she'd been thinking. Every small group was a chemistry experiment, and the procedure was always the same: bring together a group of volatile elements, put them in a tightly enclosed space, and stir. The result was never a stable compound, but sometimes you arrived at something capable of doing hard work, like a poison that killed cancer cells. And sometimes you got a bomb.

She wasn't sure what she'd created. In the first dozen meetings it was hard work just to keep everyone coming back. Stan was an expert at driving people away (he'd told her this himself). Harrison had already declared his intention to jump ship. What the members needed most was hope: hope that they could change; that they were not alone; that their suffering would ease.

With this group she was expecting a crisis call at

any time. It was a miracle that it took several months for the first one to come.

She'd been dreaming, and somehow the ringing of the phone upstairs became part of the dream. Jan was a child again, and her mother was ringing the bell that she kept beside her. Jan was terrified; she did not want to go in her mother's room. She hid in the dark, waiting for it to stop, but the ringing went on and on.

Then Jan awoke, and the dream shredded. She was in her basement. She slept down here when she had trouble falling asleep, and that had happened more and more often lately. She untangled herself from the special bed and slipped down to the cold basement floor. She made it upstairs before the phone stopped ringing.

The time and the telephone number were both a surprise: 2:20 A.M. and Mercy Hospital. The nurse told her that a patient of hers had been admitted to the ER.

"Who is it?" Jan asked, thinking: *Barbara.*

"His name is Martin Treece," the nurse said.

"Has he hurt himself?" Jan asked. Of course she thought of suicide. It was a common joke among psychotherapists that you never received crisis calls from men; you only heard from their widows.

"It's not like that," the nurse said. "He's been mugged."

Martin's glasses were gone but he still seemed to be wearing a mask. Bulging red bruises made each eye into a fist. A clear tube snaked under his swollen nose. A clamshell of bandages covered one ear. But it was his stiffness on the hospital bed—lying on his back, face pointed straight up, his bandaged left hand dead at his side atop the covers—that hinted at serious damage.

She thought he was unconscious, but then his mouth opened and he said, "Hi." The word was remarkably clear.

She moved a seat closer to the bed, being careful of the tubes and wires that sprouted from him. Martin was in a curtained-off area that was part of the ER. He hadn't been admitted to a room, and with his lack of insurance he probably wouldn't be.

"Can I get you anything?" she asked.

"The frames," he said. His hand opened. She frowned. "My *glasses*." Each "s" turned to slush. His vocal cords may have been okay, but the damage to his lips and jaw would make some consonants difficult.

She looked around the bed, then under it and the chair. Usually the hospital staff put all clothes and belongings in a clear plastic tote bag. "I don't see them," she said. "I can ask the nurses."

"I need the glasses," he said.

"I know, Martin. But I can't—"

"Buy some."

"What?"

"I'll pay you back. Or you can take them back to the store after I get mine back."

Jan sat down again. "You're going to be all right. I know you can get through this."

Without moving, Martin seemed to sink further into the bed. In his pre-group interviews, Martin insisted that his main goal for therapy was not to deal with the trauma of the murders (he could barely acknowledge that he was traumatized), but to break his dependence on the frames. He wanted to live in the world like a normal person, to stop being afraid. But losing the frames this way, Jan thought, had to be the harshest way to go cold turkey.

"Can you tell me what happened?" she asked.

"I don't remember. Not all of it."

"Then just what you can."

"I was walking home after the meeting." He spoke slowly, trying to make the words clear. "I stopped because I saw someone, then . . ." He moved slightly, signifying a shrug. "That's when they grabbed me."

"Who?"

"I don't know. They're just . . . one was in a hoodie."

She wanted to ask if they were white or black. Instead she said, "Can you describe them better?"

"They dragged me into an alley," Martin said. "It was dark. The next thing . . ." His unbandaged hand moved. "Woke up here."

"Did they rob you? Have the police made a report?" Jan asked him.

"No. I don't know. I haven't seen anyone."

"Okay, I'll contact the police and see if there's a report," Jan said. "Maybe someone saw something. In the meantime, is there anyone I can call for you? Your parents, maybe?" In the pre-group paperwork, Martin had given only one emergency number, for his parents in Minnesota.

"Please," Martin said. "Don't."

She expected that. There'd been some kind of break with his family that he'd not wanted to talk about.

"Then is there someone local we can call?"

He did not move. Perhaps he was staring at her in disbelief; it was difficult to tell.

"Okay," she said, getting frustrated. "How about your employer?"

He moved his hand again, this time in dismissal. It looked like he was trying to decide what to say.

"You can tell me," Jan said.

"Do you believe me?" he asked.

"Of course I believe you."

"No. About the frames. What I see. Do you believe what I see?"

At their first one-on-one meeting, he had told her that his greatest fear was that he was going insane. Jan said, "I've told you, Martin—I believe you."

"But *why*?" His voice was anguished. "I mean, Harrison I get. He's seen this stuff before. But you never have. You never even asked."

"I don't have to," Jan said. Later, she would regret not telling him why she did not question his "hallucinations," but at the time she thought it would interfere with the therapy. "Others have reported seeing the dwellers," she said. "I know you're not making it up."

"Good," he said. Then: "Do you know what a boss fight is?"

Jan shook her head.

"It's a gaming thing," he said. "Every game has a boss you have to fight at the end. But before you get there, you have to get through all these . . . minions."

"Okay . . ."

"I'm talking about Greta."

Jan winced inwardly. Even from his hospital bed, Martin wanted to turn Jan against her.

"The people who attacked me weren't muggers," he said. "They did this on her orders."

"*Greta's* orders?"

"She was there. In the bar where they attacked me. Meeting with Harrison. Holding hands."

"Martin, did you *follow* them?"

"One of them said, 'Don't look at her.'"

"One of the attackers? And you think they were talking about Greta?"

"They're her minions," Martin said. "Protecting her. And now they're going to come finish me."

"You don't know that."

"See?" It came out *shee?* "You don't believe me."

"You called me here to ask for my help," Jan said. "I'll do whatever I can."

"Kill the boss monster," he said.

She sat back in her seat. "I'm not going to do that."

"Didn't think so," he said. He seemed suddenly exhausted. "Just bring me my frames. I want to see them coming for me."

Jan strapped on her doctor balls and forced the staff to hunt for Martin's belongings until they turned up. The plastic bag contained Martin's clothes (bloody, torn), shoes (fine), and backpack (full of cords and batteries and a tablet computer, as well as an inside zipper pocket containing $19—she was not too bashful to check)—but the frames were not with them.

The staff's information on the police was more of a mystery; the cops were supposed to arrive "any minute now." Jan took a seat in the corridor to wait until they arrived or Martin was released; she was afraid that if Martin spoke to the cops alone, they'd soon be calling his psychologist anyway.

She knew that he was not crazy. She didn't doubt for a second the reality of his experiences. But she did doubt his conclusions.

Jan had entered all the group members' contact info into her phone. Greta had given her only one number, a cell phone. She clicked to call, then fought the urge to hang up with every chirping ring. What could she ask Greta—if she had "henchmen"?

After thirty seconds of ringing, an automated system announced that no one had set up this number for voicemail. It may not have even been Greta's real number; Jan had never had to dial it before.

She stared at the phone's screen for a while, then found another contact. After three rings a voice said, "Dr. Sayer?"

"Harrison," Jan said. "I apologize for calling so late."

"No, no, it's fine." He sounded surprisingly awake. She'd often wondered what he did with his time. On his intake form, under employment he had made a joke about being a professional "nightmarist." Then he told her he was retired. She asked him what that meant, considering he was thirty-six years old. Was he an internet millionaire? He said, "It means I stopped doing what I used to do, and haven't decided if I'm going to do anything else."

He asked, "Is there anything the matter?"

Jan told him that Martin had been attacked by several people, just a few blocks from the Elms.

"Holy shit," Harrison said. "Martin's been *attacked*?"

"They're doing more x-rays to look for more broken bones. They already think his hand is broken."

"That's terrible," Harrison said. He sounded genuinely upset. "Tell him I'm thinking of him." After a pause he said, "*Where* did this happen?" There was a new note in his voice.

"There's an Irish pub on Fourth. It was right after the meeting tonight. Last night."

The line was silent for a moment. Then: "That's why you're calling."

"Yes."

"I was there," he said. "With Greta."

"Did you see anything?" Jan asked. "Hear anything?"

But Harrison had seen nothing, even after they left the pub. He asked Jan questions, some of them the same ones as she'd asked Martin, and her answers were just as vague. She didn't mention Martin's minion theory.

"I'm looking for Greta," Jan said, moving on. "I'm not getting an answer on her phone."

He paused, then said, "Did you text her? Only old people call each other."

"But you answered."

"Exactly," he said. "Listen, I'll try her too. Is there a message you want me to pass on?"

"Just ask her to call me."

Chapter 6

We followed a strict if unconscious structure in those early meetings: We took turns, giving each a share of time to talk about our lives and deliver our spooky stories. We might as well have been sitting around a campfire.

Dr. Sayer told us this commonly happened in groups. Eventually, she said, the group would stop *telling*, and start *working*. Most of us did not know what that meant, and the rest of us pretended not to know; telling was risky enough. A crisis in the group can speed that process along, like a shock that starts the heart beating.

Martin's attack was the first of several shocks to hit the group. Barbara learned about it the next day, when Jan sent out an email to the group. Stan, who never checked his AOL account, was the last to know; Jan had left a follow-up message on his answering machine.

Harrison, of course, was the first to know. After Jan called, he hung up and sat on the bed, thinking hard.

"She's looking for me?"

He turned. Greta was sitting in the armchair across from the bed, her arms around her knees. She was still naked except for the boy's jockey shorts.

"I think she's figured out you're here," he said. "She's intuitive like that."

"So what did she say about the attackers?"

"Nothing much. Martin doesn't seem to remember, or else he didn't get a good look while they were beating him."

"I'm going to have to tell the group about the Sisters," she said.

"Yes?"

"Like you said, Jan's intuitive. She's going to ask me sooner or later. It's time to tell the story."

Harrison and Greta's relationship—their offline, out-of-band, extracurricular relationship—started after the second meeting, when she finally accepted his offer to drive her home. They barely spoke during the drive, the silence broken only by Greta's monosyllabic directions, then a final, awkward "Thanks." The next week he took her home again, and it became a regular thing. They began to talk, her short questions always aimed at getting him to talk about his childhood, and because he would not talk about that, they talked about the only thing they had in common: the group. Soon their comments became post-meeting debriefs, which became all-out dissections. The drive home became too short; they would sit in his car outside of her apartment building (a grim chunk of poured cement allocated for student use) and perform the weekly autopsy.

Harrison wasn't sure whose idea it had been to go to the pub their first time. They'd walked out of the meeting to his car and Greta said, "Maybe we could . . . ?" and Harrison said, "I know a place." And that became their new regular thing. He drank doubles of Kilbeggan. She ordered Sprite.

Greta saw things that he missed entirely. Barbara was clinically depressed, she said; you could tell in the way she talked about her family. "All her stories are about how the boys did this with their father, or did this other thing on their own. She doesn't seem to be *in* their lives. She's watching them, like they're on TV." And in the next meeting Harrison would surreptitiously study Barbara, and sure enough he would see the deep sadness behind the mask of helpfulness and empathy.

Yet in other ways, Greta was hopelessly naïve,

especially when it came to the men. For example, she'd noticed that Stan's eyes were permanently glued to her chest, but found this to be completely innocent. "He's an old man," she said. "With no hands! How does he even masturbate?"

"I'm not sure he has even the basic equipment anymore," he said. Her eyes went wide; this hadn't occurred to her. He said, "So how about Martin, then? He's got the hots for you."

"What? No. He barely looks at me."

"Because he doesn't know what to do with himself. He flushes when you come in." Later, after Martin told the group what he was seeing through the glasses, Harrison wondered if he was wrong about this.

"How about you?" she asked. "Are you looking at my tits?"

"That's beside the points. *Point.* See what I did there?"

"Everybody thinks I'm the quiet one," she said. "But you're the one who never talks."

"I do so. I talk all the time."

"No, you *comment.* What have you shared about yourself? We don't know you, we just know that guy in the books." She always turned the conversation back around to the paperbacks. "Jameson Squared," she said. "Monster Detective."

"And that is such a misleading title," he said. "It

makes the kid sound like he's the monster. Like 'child psychologist.'"

"Child psychologists *are* monsters," she said.

"No, I mean—"

"I know what you mean. Jesus, Harrison."

"Now that would be a good series character. Jesus Harrison, Divine Detective."

"You also deflect through humor," Greta said.

Every pub session, after they'd finished diagnosing the problems of the other people in the group (including Dr. Sayer), Greta would hound him about the books, trying to nail down what was real, what was made up, what was only exaggerated. She seemed to have memorized the entire series.

The mundane facts—the NPR facts, he called them—were that the town of Dunnsmouth was reduced to kindling by a hurricane. Hundreds dead. It was quite a story for perhaps a week, and then the world moved on. Then, two years after the tragedy, a wife-and-husband team of "paranormal investigators" published a "nonfiction" book about the true, unreported supernatural intrusion that was only *interpreted* as a hurricane. One of the main characters was a teenage boy, the transparently named Jameson Jameson. Harrison had made the very bad mistake of talking to the couple while he was recovering in the hospital. Soon after, he made it a life goal to someday punch the paranormal investigators in their pair of normal faces. The list of punchees later expanded, first to the editors at Macmillan who ginned up a "fictional-but-what-if-it's-not-eh?" series of adventures featuring a character named Jameson Squared, then to the producers at the Sci-Fi (now SyFy) network who created a homegrown movie he would have called unwatchable if so many people hadn't told him they'd watched it.

"You can't blame people for wanting to tell your story," Greta said. "You're a hero."

"That's bullshit," he said.

"Not total bullshit," she said.

"You're an optimist. Let's agree that the glass is half full of shit."

"You saved an entire town!"

"If by 'saving' you mean that slightly fewer people died than every single fucking person, sure. Totally saved it."

"That's not what—"

"Dunnsmouth was a clusterfuck, top to bottom," he said. "The books don't tell you how close we came to losing everything. I was seventeen, Greta. I didn't know what the hell I was doing, and I didn't know how far out of control the situation was. Everyone should have died. Not just everyone in town—*every-one*."

She stared at him.

"I'm not being dramatic," he said. "Okay, maybe a

little. I'm sure there would have been a few survivors, somewhere. But not on the eastern seaboard."

"But that didn't happen," she said. "You must have done something right."

"Sometimes fortune favors the stupid."

She shook her head. "You keep doing that. Making quips."

"'Quips'? Who says 'quips'?"

"Mocking quips is also a quip." She frowned. "And trust me—I am *not* an optimist."

On the June night Martin was beaten, Harrison and Greta had left the meeting and walked to the pub as usual. They did not notice that Martin was following them. Greta was upset that Martin kept pressuring her for details.

"He has a point," Harrison said. "You know what happened to the rest of us. It's your turn."

"I'm not interested in taking turns."

She had already told him fragments of her story. She'd grown up on some kind of all-female commune out West; they called themselves the Unveiled Sisters at first, then just the Sisters. She'd been raised by her mother; Dad was some variety of asshole who'd not been part of her life since she was very small.

Greta said, "Martin just wants to know about the scars. And the monster."

"I'm assuming they're related." He retrieved their

drinks. After they'd taken their first sips, he said, "So. The scars."

She stared at him.

He said, "Are you afraid I won't believe you? Because I can promise you there's no shit too weird for me." He put his hand over hers. "Nothing you say can scare me off."

Greta seemed to move without moving. He jerked backward, chair legs squealing. For a moment she became, somehow, more *real*. He felt suddenly naked. Like prey.

He'd yanked his hand away from her, and he tried to cover by rubbing the back of his neck. He'd experienced flashes like these before, these intimations of the hidden world, but he could never predict when they'd hit, and they never lasted for longer than a second or two. For that he was thankful. Seers like Martin had a shitty time of it.

"Or," he said, putting on a smile, "maybe you can."

"Drive me home," she said. Then: "Not *my* home."

Harrison's apartment was the latest in a string of apartments, and though he had lived there for two years, he'd not finished unpacking. Barely started, actually. He'd set up his laptop and some speakers on the dining room table, but his books were still in boxes. The kitchen cabinets were empty. He had managed to set out a few special items on the shelves in the living room, mementos from his childhood. Photos of his parents. A few hand-carved stone statues from the bottom of Dunnsmouth Bay. A framed copy of his high school diploma, still stained with blotches of black ichor. A skull that looked like a goat's skull but was not.

Greta moved around the room, looking at them with undisguised curiosity. She stared for a long time at the picture of his mother and father and the three-year-old Harrison, squinting into the sunlight on a California beach. She ran her hands along the shelves. "Is this *gold*?" she said, hefting a disc the size of her palm. The edges of it looked as if they'd been chewed, and the thing on its face was no human king or president.

"It's harder to spend than you think," Harrison said. "I suppose I could melt it down."

"Right." She returned it to the shelf, then stood with her back to him. "So you're squatting here?"

"Hey!"

"No sheets on the bed, empty Scotch bottles on the counter. Even the carpet smells like liquor."

"If you want to leave," he said. "I can drive you back."

"Sit," she said, and gestured toward the bed. She moved six feet away from him and pulled off her long-sleeved T-shirt. Underneath she wore a thin white wife-beater. She peeled that off as well.

"Oh," he said. He hadn't meant to speak aloud. He didn't want to spook her. And he thought he'd been prepared for this; she'd shown her arm in one of the earliest meetings. But this . . .

The scars covered her from the base of her neck and continued past the waistline of her jeans. The swirls and nested blocks he'd seen on her arms were even more closely packed across her chest, more dense than a Mondrian painting, crowded as an Escher maze. Even her breasts—compact runner's breasts— were covered in ridges and sworls.

She shook her head at him. He didn't know what that gesture meant, or even if it was directed at him. Then she unzipped her jeans and stepped out of them. She left on her underwear, small gray boy shorts with a black waistband, and kicked off her Chuck Taylors. There was a moment of awkwardness as she bent to peel off her black athletic socks. Then she stood.

The scars scrolled down each leg, swarmed her feet, wound through her toes. She weathered his gaze with eyes open.

After a time she turned to show him her back. No space larger than a couple of inches had been left unfilled. She was a Torah, a labyrinth.

"The Sisters gave me my first brand when I was seven years old," she said. She turned again, and showed him a tiny square on her left bicep. "This. It was my birthday. I was so happy."

"Happy," he said skeptically.

"My mother had already decorated herself with beautiful designs," Greta said. "They were tattoos, not scars, and nothing . . . mystical. But so full of color. I remember tracing them, my nose so close to her skin, staring at the pictures so hard I thought I'd fall in. On her left arm was a tattoo of an ivy-covered gate. I thought that if I looked close enough between the bars I could see to the other side. God, I loved them. She added to her collection pretty frequently. Sometimes she let me come with. This was before we joined the Sisters, before we left my dad, when I was little. I remember the hum of the needles, the tiny pinpricks of blood. Once I asked if it hurt, and she said, Of course it does, honey. Everything beautiful hurts."

"That's kind of fucked up," Harrison said.

"Tell me it's not true," she said. Without waiting for a response she said, "This one they gave me a few days later."

Over the next hour she guided him through a tour of her body, though she never let him come closer than a few feet to her. Her skin was both the map and the territory: She told him how and when she acquired each brand, and how much she loved the Sisters. "This one took weeks to heal," she said. "It felt like the whole summer."

She was talking about a jagged design near her

navel. Looking at it made him queasy. "I know that symbol," he said.

Her eyes narrowed.

"And that one, on your leg. And there was another on your back—two, I think. Related."

"How?" she asked. "Where have you seen them?"

"The other side."

"What does that *mean*?"

"That I was over there?" he asked.

"That they're on *me*."

"I don't know yet."

Harrison's cell phone buzzed. He glanced at the screen—not many people had this number—and then picked it up. A few minutes later he hung up and told Greta that she would have to tell them about the Sisters. "The doctor and Martin, at least."

"Might as well be the whole group," Greta said.

"Yeah," he said heavily. Then: "You can probably keep your clothes on, though."

He said it jokingly, but suddenly she was embarrassed. She came out of the chair and started scooping up her clothes.

"Where are you going?" he asked. "Are you leaving?"

She wouldn't answer him. He said, "What happened to the Sisters, Greta? Are they still out there?"

"They're dead." She pulled on one of her shoes. "All dead. *Whoosh*."

She finished dressing, then stared at him, hands on hips.

"What?" he asked.

"I still need a ride," she said.

Chapter 7

At the next meeting we were all shocked by Martin's appearance, in both senses of the word "appearance": shocked at the bruises and bandages, and shocked that he had come to the group at all. He looked like a zombie from his video game: his face misshapen by the beating, still swollen in yellow and purple. One arm was in a cast from wrist to elbow, and the fingers themselves were wrapped, making it look like one of Stan's stumps.

Jan had tried to tell him that he did not need to come to the meeting, and she'd understand if he wanted to drop out entirely. She would see him in solo therapy if that's what he wanted. But no, Martin was determined to attend. He needed to see the others, and he needed to be seen.

"God *damn*, kid!" Stan said. "God *damn*!"

Martin put down his bulging backpack and took

his seat next to Barbara. She touched his shoulder and said, "I'm so sorry. How are you holding up?"

He didn't know how to answer that question. He was upright, so was that holding up? His body ached. His bones felt as shaky as Tinkertoys. Even under this blanket of Vicodin—he was still taking four a day—spikes of pain would shoot up his spine with no warning. When he turned his head too fast, his vision swam.

Oh, and the world without frames. It was so strange to see without filters—to see this group without protection. The only advantage was that he could almost forget that Greta was a monster.

"I also need to find a new place to crash," Martin said.

"Why's that?" Harrison asked.

"I got kicked out," Martin said, which was not a lie. He kept the explanation vague, making it seem like a problem about money and roommates. Only Jan knew the whole story.

Stan, though, was still outraged on Martin's behalf. "You can't kick a man out of his home!"

"Where are you going to live?" Barbara asked.

"I'll think of something," he said.

Harrison said, "If you need some help—"

"From *you*?" Martin said.

Harrison started to say something, then seemed to think better of it. He glanced at Jan as if asking her permission to proceed. "Dr. Sayer told me that Martin was attacked right outside the bar where Greta and I were talking. We'd met there several times. After almost every meeting, actually."

Stan raised his eyebrows.

"To talk," Harrison said.

"Uh-huh," Stan said.

"I—*we* should have told the group. I apologize for that. If we'd been more open, then maybe—"

"Maybe I wouldn't have stalked you," Martin said.

"You really did that?" Barbara asked him.

"She left *wakes*," Martin said. "Ripples in the air."

"Really?" Stan said.

"Yup."

Barbara said to Martin, "Do you want to talk about the attack?"

"No," Martin said. He looked at Greta: straight on, from beneath eyelids puffy from the beating. "I want *her* to talk about it."

"The cut was very small," Greta said. "Maybe an inch long."

Her voice was so quiet. Martin leaned forward, thinking, Finally.

"The razor was so sharp I didn't feel it."

Barbara made a noise, a tiny intake of breath, and Martin looked up. The woman's eyes shone with unshed tears. What was going on with her? he wondered. In the first meetings Barbara had been so composed, knees together and voice calm, as polished as a Nordstrom's saleslady.

Greta said, "All I remember was the ice cube the Sisters rubbed over my arm first. Then one of the other elders distracted me, making faces, and when I looked down they were placing a thin piece of gauze in the wound."

"*In* the wound?" Barbara asked.

"You twist the gauze, like you're rolling a joint, then you lay it in there. They have to keep open. The skin has to raise before scarring. You cut the skin of a child, you have to be careful or they'll heal up without a trace." She said this matter-of-factly. "Every successful brand comes from delayed healing."

Greta described how the cuttings proceeded, from tiny incisions to longer, more intricate designs. They concentrated at first on her arms, then legs, so that she could see them. "The Sisters wanted me to love them as much as they did."

"The sisters, the *sisters*," Stan said. "What the hell kind of sister would do this?"

Martin almost laughed. Stan was the king of outrage.

"*The* Sisters," Greta said, and then Stan heard it the way they did: a proper noun, capitalization required.

"I was related to only one of them," she said. "My mother. It was kind of a commune."

"In the what—the nineties? Who the hell still lives on a commune?"

"It was Oregon," Greta said.

But Stan was steamrolling now. "Well where the hell were your teachers? Your neighbors? Didn't anybody notice they were cutting up a little kid? You weren't in God damn Africa."

"I was homeschooled," Greta said evenly. "All the daughters were. The Sisters were self-sufficient. Everything we needed was on the farm, and the only time I saw outsiders was when I helped set up our stand at the farmers' market, or when the fuel-oil truck came."

"That's terrible," Barbara said.

"No! I loved it there," Greta said. "And the Sisters loved me. More than they did the other girls."

Stan said, "You're telling us this commune was all women?"

The old man's voice had a strange tone to it. You old perv, Martin thought.

"She's telling us that she was in a cult," Harrison said.

"It's more complicated than that," Greta said.

"It always seems that way," Martin said. "From the inside."

Greta jerked in her seat. Martin saw the monster

erupt in her, flashing white-orange like the mouth of a blast furnace. He grunted in pain. The light had brought tears to his eyes.

He didn't understand what had happened. He wasn't wearing the frames.

Greta said, "You don't know what you're talking about."

Martin held up a hand. He was still seeing spots. "I'm sorry, I'm sorry . . ." When he looked up, Harrison was staring at him, his eyes narrowed as if measuring the space between them.

"You okay, Martin?" Harrison asked.

"I'm fine," Martin said.

"So are you still in it?" Stan asked Greta. "This cult?"

Jan said, "I don't think it's helpful to keep using that word."

"It's over," Greta said. "When I was sixteen, there was a fire. An old bus was parked too close to the main house. The bus caught fire, and that spread . . ." She shook her head. "Everything fell apart after that. There were news stories. The survivors turned on each other. The whole community disbanded." She grimaced. "I know the farm wasn't perfect, but I still miss it."

"Wasn't *perfect*?" Stan said sarcastically. "They cut you!"

Jan said, "Greta, you said the Sisters loved you more than the other girls. How so?"

"All the daughters were marked on their seventh birthday. Then again every month, just tiny little cuts. We were all trying to get our first square. But I wanted more. I *asked* for more. The other girls dropped out one by one. But I kept going."

The designs became more elaborate, the cuts deeper. By the time she was thirteen, she told the group, all the other girls had dropped out, and Greta was the sole object of the elders' attention. The scars covered her arms and legs. She ached constantly. Her skin wept blood. Some mornings after a ritual she woke to find herself glued to the bed, skin and bandages and T-shirt and sheet transformed into one thing, cemented by blood. But still she wouldn't stop.

She had her first period while laid out on a table, naked from the waist up. The elder women were carving the next ring of a spiraling symbol into her stomach, and they cried with joy when they saw the spots in her underwear. They stopped early that day, but the remaining sessions were longer. She was a woman now.

"I could take the pain," she said. "I was the *queen* of pain. I got so I could breathe through any session, two hours, three. Sometimes I felt like I was floating above the table. I felt like I was opening myself to something greater."

Greta paused, and Martin risked a glance at her.

She was smiling shyly. She said, "They told me I would be worshiped."

"And you *believed* them?" Stan asked.

"They were already worshiping me," Greta said. "Every time they put the knife to my skin it was like . . ." She shook her head. "I don't know."

"A prayer," Barbara said.

"Yes," Greta said. "Like that."

The elders talked to her while they cut, telling her stories of the Hidden Ones. These were creatures in exile, cousins to angels, who wanted to reenter the world. Greta—little Greta!—was the key to opening that door. The symbols that she wore were like candles to their more fierce flames. Like to like, they said.

The sessions continued—once a month, twice at most, because the wounds needed time to ripen into high-ridged scars. The weeks of recovery were harder than the cut days. She constantly ran a low-grade fever. Antibiotics accompanied every meal. Some days she never left the cabin she shared with her mother.

Then Greta had to explain to the group that it was not really a cabin, but a rusting VW camper van, immobile for a decade, squatting in high grass. It was clean, though, and dry, and she and her mother were happy to have it. The Sisters had taken in Greta's mother when she was running from her boyfriend, a dangerous man. This was not an unusual story at the farm. Many of the women were hiding from dangerous men: husbands, boyfriends, fathers. The founders of the farm, back in the '70s, were three Middle Eastern women who fled first their marriages, then mainstream Islam. They had decided upon a different course. They welcomed other women, of all races and religions, and slowly introduced them to the mysteries of the Hidden Ones.

One night the fever climbed, and she couldn't sleep. She tore at the bedclothes, crying. Then suddenly a man was standing beside the bed. A man, but also a column of smokeless flame; both those things at once. He was beautiful. His eyes were half lidded, his lips slightly parted. The flame pulsed with his breath. He frightened her, and aroused her. She opened her legs to him, but he refused to come any closer. She thrashed and wailed. Still he wouldn't move.

In the morning, when Greta told her mother what she'd seen, her mother burst into tears and ran to tell the elders. The news spread instantly. When Greta walked through the farm to the showers, the women and children stared at her.

"I felt like a rock star," Greta told the group. "And then it got weird."

"Ohhh," Stan said. "*Then* it got weird."

A few weeks after her sixteenth birthday, the mood at the farm changed. The elders whispered just out of earshot, and studied her with worried expressions. Then she overheard her mother pleading with one of the elders, saying, She's not ready, she's too young.

Greta was worried, but not scared. She'd been raised up in full knowledge of her uniqueness—she was *made* unique. Still, she didn't demand that the elders tell her what was going on. She would not ask even her mother—at least in public.

"That night I confronted my mother," Greta said. "I asked her, Is it happening? Is it finally happening? And my mother broke down. Started crying. She kept saying, They can't make you, I'll help you get away."

Greta shook her head. "I think I laughed at her. I know I felt like laughing. Because why would I ever leave? This was my home. This was where I was loved. But my mother was so upset. She took my hands and said, 'Aunty Siddra is dying. She's coming here to perform the ceremony.'"

"Did I miss something?" Stan said. "Who the hell is Aunty Siddra? Was *what* finally happening?"

"My wedding day," Greta said.

Silence crackled like a static charge.

Then Stan asked: "To who?"

"The human torch guy," Martin said.

That only exasperated Stan more. "But what does that have to do with her scars?"

Greta started to answer, and Harrison said, "They were trying to make her look attractive to something from the other side." He glanced at Greta and she held his gaze for a moment, then looked down.

"That's what you were seeing before," Harrison said to Martin. "She's not a monster. She's monster bait."

The convoy (Greta told them, her voice soft but insistent) arrived in the afternoon, grinding and thumping through the potholes in the gravel road. First a boxy sedan with a cracked window, then a pickup truck with a blue tarp flapping over the bed, and last a school bus. Or rather, a former school bus; this one was hand-painted in reds and oranges, obliterating the yellow and black. The three vehicles drove up to the farmhouse and parked in a semi-circle before it. The bus seemed somehow larger than the house, and instantly became the capital of their little community.

Half a dozen women emerged from the pickup and car, smiling and stretching. They were dark-haired women in jeans and T-shirts, some in head scarves. Sisters came hurrying in from the fields, and the elders called out names, drew the visitors into hugs.

Greta watched from the periphery. The bus door

did not open. A figure moved behind the wide windshield, another dark-haired woman who reached up and tugged the curtains closed. Greta realized the vehicle was a kind of RV. Most of the bus's side windows had been filled in, and the rest were curtained. The roof was piled with luggage.

Her mother called Greta's name, and the girl stepped nervously forward. The visitors exchanged looks, then one of the women approached Greta, holding out her hands. Greta didn't know what to do, so she held out her own hands, and the woman laughed and took them in her own. "Little sister," the woman said, and suddenly the rest of the visitors were surrounding her, touching her, laughing with her.

Finally they withdrew, and the elders moved off into the farmhouse. The bus remained sealed, its engine keeping up its watchdog rumble. Was Aunty too ill to leave? Greta's mother had said she was dying. How old *was* the woman? Greta had heard stories about her since she was a child. Siddra was the only surviving member of the three original founders. She lived somewhere far away, and Greta had imagined a mansion, a fortress, a treehouse. Anything but this ramshackle bus.

All that afternoon Greta never strayed far from the vehicle, her eyes moving between the side door and that big curtained window. No one entered or exited.

Her mother came back to the cabin very late, and Greta pretended to be asleep. Her mother stood over her in the dark, breathing. Greta watched her silhouette through half-lidded eyes.

Then her mother knelt beside the mattress. Her clothes smelled of some strange spice. She touched Greta on her hip. "Oh," her mother said quietly. "Oh my daughter."

She was going to try to talk her out of it, Greta thought. She held her body still. If she waited long enough, her mother would give up.

Then her mother said, almost breathing it, "You are so lucky."

The next morning, her mother set out a pretty, pale green dress that still had the JCPenney tags. Greta stood very still at the bathroom mirror as her mother combed her hair and—a first—applied mascara to her eyelashes. "Pout," her mother said, and touched Greta's lips with coral lipstick.

Together they walked to the center of the farm. Greta resisted the urge to take her mother's hand. The fields around them were empty, but sisters stood on the porch of the main house, or in the doorways of their campers and cabins.

Greta and her mother stopped in front of the bus, looking up at the door. Nothing happened. Greta glanced at her mom, and then the door of the bus folded open. One of the dark-haired women from last night stood at the top of the stairs beside the driver's seat, holding the metal handle of the lever with a cloth, as if it were an oven mitt. She smiled and gestured for her to come in.

Greta stepped up. The inside of the bus was twenty degrees hotter than outside. The dark-haired woman was sweating.

Greta realized her mother hadn't stepped up after her. "You're not coming?" Greta asked. She tried to keep her voice calm.

Her mother's lips were pursed, her eyes gleaming. "I'll wait for you here," her mother said. "Go on."

The bus door closed. The dark-haired woman touched Greta on the shoulder, then gestured for her to sit in a chair in the middle of the room. The woman walked past her to a wall made of faux wood paneling that did not quite meet the curve of the roof. A curtain covered a doorway, and the woman disappeared behind it.

Greta smoothed out her dress and controlled her breathing as if preparing for a new cut. Everything in the room seemed to be wrapped in layers; couches covered in colored sheets piled with blankets topped by pillows; scarves over purple lamp shades over tinted bulbs; rugs askew atop other rugs. Color upon color upon color. The air too was almost liquid with incense and wood smoke and the smell of strong coffee.

Too much. Too much.

She began to sweat. In front of her was a low cloth-draped table, perhaps a storage trunk, upon which were set nine or ten candles, burning in small glass cups of green and purple and yellow. The little flames seemed to fill up the room with heat. On the other side of the table was a huge armchair that Greta assumed belonged to Aunty Siddra. The arms of the chair had once been upholstered, but now they were bare wood, scorched black. The velour seat cushions, however, looked new.

The curtain moved, and it was as if an oven door had opened. Hot air swept over her and made her shrink in her chair.

Aunty Siddra appeared. She was a collection of spikes and angles, like a burnt tree still standing after a forest fire. And she was marked, too. Candlelight limned every ridge and scar.

Greta started to get to her feet and the old woman waved for her to sit down. She moved slowly, as if her limbs might snap under her own weight. She settled into her throne-like chair one bone at a time.

The woman wore a sleeveless shirt and a skirt that hung to her knees, so arms and hands and shin bones were visible. Every inch of visible skin mirrored Greta's; the designs were the same. They were two copies of the same document, penned decades apart.

No, not copies. Not exactly. The woman's forehead was branded, where Greta's was unmarked. The top scars made a jagged line, as if a serrated knife had sawed away at her skull, and that line curved inward at each end.

Aunty Siddra smiled. "Candy?"

"Pardon?"

The woman held out a glass bowl full of what looked like dusty marbles. "Go on," she said.

Greta did not want any candy, but she took a reddish brown lump. The surface felt crusty, like a sugar cube. She held it to her nose, then put it in her mouth. It tasted of some spice she didn't recognize, like licorice but not.

Aunty smiled as if she'd trapped the girl. "I bet you don't get much candy in this shit hole," she said.

"Not much," Greta agreed.

Aunty popped a candy into her mouth. "I didn't expect a white girl. But I guess vanilla is the hot new flavor."

Greta didn't know what to say to that.

"Do you know why you're here?" Aunty Siddra asked.

"I think so."

"Hmm." The woman leaned back. "Guess my age." When Greta said nothing she said, "Go on. Don't be shy. Sixty-five? Seventy?"

Greta shook her head.

"I'm fifty-two," she said. "Fifty-*two*." She looked at the ceiling.

Greta sat still for a minute, two. Suddenly Aunty Siddra looked at her. "There was supposed to be a revolution. We were supposed to form our own society. And the Hidden Ones would be our nuclear deterrent. You know what a nuclear deterrent is?"

Greta nodded, though she wasn't quite sure.

"Yeah, well, the revolution's always around the corner. We just wanted to have our weapon in place. And once we made our deal with foreign powers—well, you know, don't you? One from our side, one from theirs."

"'A bridge and a bond,'" Greta quoted from her lessons.

"Right," Aunty Siddra said. "But that doesn't mean you have to do everything the other guy says." She sat up straighter. "Listen to me, this is important. Don't ever let go. Hold tight to the reins. You can do this, yes? Because we need a woman who won't flinch, who can *take* it. Who can hold on to that son of a bitch, no matter how much it makes you hurt." She gripped the sides of the chair. "Are you that woman?"

"Yes," Greta said. "I am."

"Thank God," Aunty Siddra said. "I don't think I can hold out much longer."

———

A final step was required, Greta told the group. She was to come back in an hour after they prepared the bus for the surgery. Back in her cabin, she stared at her face in the bathroom mirror. She ran a finger across her smooth forehead, saying goodbye to it. Her mother pestered her with questions she didn't know how to answer. What was Aunty Siddra like? Was she nice? Did she approve of Greta?

Greta shut the bathroom door on her mother and sat down on the closed lid of the toilet. She was sick to her stomach, and her skin felt clammy.

Before the hour was up, a neighbor came to their camper and banged on the door. "Something's wrong," she said.

A crowd had gathered around the bus. The door was open, and dark-haired women were hurrying in and out. Greta went in without asking for permission. Aunty Siddra lay on the couch. She was not moving. One of the women sat cross-legged on the floor, holding her hand.

"What's the matter with her?" Greta asked.

"Cancer, child. It's all through her."

"But—but what about. . . ?"

"Sit." She pointed to the huge chair Aunty Siddra had occupied less than an hour ago. Greta did as she was told. She put a hand down on the chair arm, then quickly lifted it; the arms were coated with black soot.

The dark-haired woman said, "Someone get the knives. Hurry!"

But it was too late. Aunty Siddra had taken her last breath.

"And then. . . ." Greta told us. "The fire."

"I was the only one who made it out of the bus," Greta said. "I crawled out, between the legs of the women. The fire seemed to jump from Sister to Sister. And then it spread to the farmhouse, the other outbuildings."

"I don't understand," Barbara said. "Where did the fire come from?"

"It was the Hidden One," Greta said. "Aunty Siddra had let go of the reins, and it was free."

"They fucked it up," Harrison said. "They didn't complete the ritual. They were supposed to move the thing from the old lady to Greta—one bottle to another. But they didn't get it done before the first bottle broke."

"What are you talking about, bottles?" Martin asked.

"You know what they call 'hidden one' in Arabic?" Harrison said. "*Al-jinnī.*"

Martin thought for a moment, then got it. "Oh come on!"

"It's just a word for something they don't understand. It's not Barbara Eden, or Robin fucking Williams."

"We're already out of time," Jan said. "Next week we can—"

"*Nobody move*," Martin said.

Harrison and Barbara looked toward Jan.

"Please," Martin said.

"What is it?" Jan asked him. "What do you have to say?"

Martin turned his broken face to Greta. "So. These Sisters. They thought you were special."

Greta nodded.

"Special enough to kill for?"

"Oh," Barbara said. And Stan said, "What?"

"The people who attacked me," Martin said. "Some of them were women, I'm pretty sure. Maybe all of them. And they were protecting Greta."

"There *are* no Sisters," Greta said. "The fire killed everyone. Everyone but me."

No one spoke. Martin saw that Harrison was staring at the floor, lost in thought.

Most of us were watching either Martin or Greta. Jan, however, was watching Harrison. He was staring into the middle distance with a thoughtful look on his face.

"End of story," Greta said. She looked at Martin. "Happy now?"

He wasn't happy. But he was satisfied.

Chapter 8

We knew each other, at first, only by our words. We sat in a circle and spoke to each other, presenting some version of ourselves. We told our stories and tried out behaviors. Dr. Sayer said that the group was the place for "reality testing." What would happen if we exposed ourselves and shared our true thoughts? What if we talked about what we most feared? What if we behaved according to rules that were not predicated on our worst suspicions?

Perhaps the world would not end.

For Stan, the group was his opportunity to test the assumption that every living person was repulsed by him. Decades of personal experience had convinced him of this. Understandably, he'd taken the position that the best defense was being offensive. He shouted at medical staff. He accused doctors of minimizing his problems before they could even hear his complaints. He stared at people on the street, daring them to look away.

Being a psychologically savvy person, he knew that the others might perceive his house as an expression of his inner defense mechanisms. He'd grown up in this house, and had returned to it after his experience with the Weavers. It was his castle, his fortress, and defended by palisades of junk. Every room was filled, with narrow paths winding through the piles of broken appliances, books, clothing, children's toys, lawn equipment. Only the Medicaid-paid staff dared enter, and they didn't stay long; home health workers were on the lowest rung of the medical economy and they didn't collect hazard pay.

Dr. Sayer, had she known about his living conditions, would have been more likely to reach for the DSM-5 for a label; hoarding was a cousin to OCD and its victims sometimes responded to SSRIs. A steady dose of Paxil could do wonders in a small minority of patients.

Stan, however, knew that the house was not his problem, people were.

So it was that he'd surprised himself by inviting Martin to spend a night or two there, "just until he found a new place." The invitation had been Barbara's idea. She'd cornered him after the meeting in which Greta had told her story, just to "brainstorm." She played upon his conscience, daring him to help someone in greater need than himself. "Mentor him," she'd said. Of course, she'd never been to his house either.

Martin regretted accepting the invitation almost as much as Stan regretted offering it. There was something about Barbara, however, that made him want to be a better person. Perhaps it was because she seemed to think he was, despite very little evidence, already a good person. Both Martin and Stan didn't want to disappoint her.

Stan's driver, the bearded young man who seemed about the same age as Martin, said, "You're *staying* with him?" He shook his head in disbelief, and when he unlocked the door to the house he chuckled in a low voice that reminded Martin of every cafeteria bully he'd known in middle school. "Enjoy your stay."

Martin shut the door behind them. "What an asshole." Then he looked up to see the condition of the room.

For a long moment he couldn't think of anything to say.

Stan suddenly seemed angry. He gestured at the goat path through the mess and said, "Kitchen's through there."

"Got it," Martin said, and began to push Stan's

chair—slowly, and with many small corrections. His cast made it difficult. And still he couldn't think what to say about the house. He was appalled but also fascinated. The way through the maze of the front room was like a series of D&D traps, set with hair triggers and hidden pressure plates. Move a broken microwave off a stack of *National Geographic*s and a boulder might burst through the wall and flatten them.

Martin thought about bugging out as soon as possible, but where else could he go? His checking account was down to gravel and his credit card had been scraped clean by the hospital and pharmacy. He needed to go back to work, to get looking for a new place to live, but the thought exhausted him. The beating had beaten something out of him. What had been lost, however, was a mystery; Stan would have called it gumption, or resilience. To Martin it felt like he'd sloughed off some other, tougher self, leaving behind a fragile pupa. All he wanted to do was sleep.

But that was looking to be impossible in Stan's house. There was hardly any space to lie down, and nowhere to even sit safely. They passed a door that was ajar, but behind it was a wall of floor-to-ceiling crap like a dead end in a closed-environment game level. The kitchen was a wreck, full of non-food-related junk. Why was there a black safe sitting atop the stove?

Martin said, "I don't know, Stan, maybe I should—"

"Try upstairs," Stan said. He pointed at twin pillars of boxes. Between them was a narrow opening.

Martin slipped into the gap and discovered a set of stairs that led to a miracle: three bedrooms and a tiny bathroom, empty except for an appropriate amount of furniture. The rooms were dusty but not dirty; someone, at least in the past couple months, had cleaned them. This was higher ground, saved from the floodwaters of Stan's compulsion by the lack of a ramp or chair lift.

Martin returned to the first floor, moving slowly so as not to aggravate his ribs. Stan looked at him expectantly.

Martin wanted to say, This is the first time I've been thankful for lack of handicap accessibility. Instead he said, "This is perfect. Thanks."

"You'll be safe here," Stan said. "You wouldn't believe how many guns I have."

Greta didn't show up for the next meeting. She'd sent Jan a text saying that she needed to work on something on her own. The tone, Jan told them, did not seem to rule out an eventual return; but when Jan texted her back, she got no further reply.

It was left to the group to deal with her departure. It was a rejection, a wound. We spent three weeks talking about it, assessing the damage, assigning blame. Martin thought Greta was a coward. Stan thought she was striking back at them for forcing her to talk. Harrison thought she just needed a break from the group and would be back when she needed them. Barbara, however, refused to take Greta's exit as a sign of aggression *or* weakness. "Maybe she got what she needed," Barbara said. "The group's job is to patch us up so we're strong enough to go do what we need to do. We're not supposed to be here forever."

What surprised us—the remaining members, that is, if not Dr. Sayer—was that we were *able* to talk about it so deeply and so well. Dr. Sayer seemed to do very little; she made comments that would nudge our little boat back into the stream and we would do the rowing ourselves. When we fell back into storytelling—and Stan was still our most frequent offender—one of us would nudge us back into the now. What mattered was what happened between us.

One week he was talking again about his time with the Weavers, the days he spent in that barn, in the nest of ropes that stretched between the rafters and the poles. He seemed to remember every kindness that the Pest, the smallest Weaver, had done for him, even as he watched his friends die, one by one. "Their mistake was killing the cop. If Bertram Weaver hadn't had done that, they would never have found me. I would have made my last visit to the smokehouse. But the cops burst in, and Bertram tried to rush them—"

"Stan, you've told this story before," Barbara said. "When you go on and on like that, it's like you're demanding that I tune you out. The more you talk, the less I can hear you."

Stan lifted the oxygen mask, inhaled deeply. We'd seen this delaying tactic before. Often it ended any meaningful interaction with the old man. But this time he lowered the mask and said, "Then you've trapped me. If I talk you don't listen, and if I don't talk . . . what am I supposed to do?"

"Tell us something you've never told before," Barbara said. "Something real. How do you feel, right now?"

"I feel sorry," Stan said. "I don't mean to bore you. I don't know why I do that. I just . . . fill the room."

"I'm more concerned about what you're not saying," Barbara said.

"Are there things you're not telling us?" Martin asked.

"Of course there are," Harrison said. "We all have secrets left."

"Whenever you're ready, Harrison," Barbara said.

Harrison laughed. "I'll let you know."

Despite Greta's absence, a lightness seemed to have entered the meetings. The gloom around Barbara (which only Jan and Greta had noticed) had lifted.

Martin seemed to be healing. He was still living with Stan, but he'd gone back to work, thanks to a phone call and earnest letter from Dr. Sayer. He told the group he was adjusting to life without the frames. He knew the dwellers were lurking just out of sight, and he never forgot that, but he could function *as if* there were no dwellers. "I just tell myself to act like they're not there," Martin said one week. "And sometimes I can fool even myself."

"Amen," Harrison said. "That's my primary maintenance strategy."

"How so?" Jan asked.

"You know. Act normal. Pretend we don't know what we know. But it's so . . . tiring. I start to hate people for their ignorance. Their complacency. Sometimes I see a couple people sitting around laughing and I think, What the fuck do you think is so funny?"

The rest of us were nodding. Even Jan.

"I want to be like them. But I can't. We're not safe. There are things on the other side that want in—the dwellers, the Hidden Ones. And scarier shit."

"They whisper," Martin said.

"Yes," Harrison said. "Always trying to get someone to open the door."

"Like Aunty Siddra," Barbara said.

"And the Weavers," Stan said.

"Well, the Weavers were just psychos, right?" Harrison said. "Nothing like the thing that burned down Greta's farm."

Stan said, "I do *not* agree with that."

"I'm not saying they weren't scary," Harrison said. "But they didn't bring over monsters."

"They wanted to become the monsters," Jan said. She sounded almost angry.

Harrison looked at the others, seeing if they'd noticed her tone.

"And they got halfway there," Jan said. She looked up. "Stan, tell them about the Spidermother."

Stan flinched as if he'd been slapped. Tears filled his eyes. He opened his mouth to speak, then closed it.

"It's okay, dear," Barbara said. "What is it?"

But Stan was staring at Dr. Sayer. "How do you know about that?"

"It was in the police reports."

"Back up," Martin said. "*Spider*mother?"

"That's what her boys called her." Stan rubbed at his eyes with his sleeve. "Mrs. Weaver. That's who they were feeding."

"Fuck," Harrison said.

"They kept her in the smokehouse," Stan said. "They were afraid of her, but they loved her too. She looked . . . pregnant. Or like those starving kids in Africa, with the big distended bellies? The rest of her, her arms and legs, were like sticks. And filthy.

But the worst part was her eyes. There was something wrong with her eyes. She had too many of them."

Martin bent forward in his chair. "What?!"

"Inside her sockets. She had two in each socket. Small, shiny black . . . spider eyes."

"Another fucking hybrid," Harrison said. The rest of us looked at him. "If something's made it across, it can taint people. And their children. You get things that shouldn't exist."

"The Scrimshander," Barbara said. "Half dweller, half human."

"Yeah, him," Harrison said. "And others."

"But you killed it, right?" Martin asked.

Harrison shrugged. "Probably. Other people thought they killed it too. It's hundreds of years old. It may not *be* killable."

"What are you saying?" Stan said. He was frantic. "The Spidermother may still be alive? They burned her out. The whole place went down. I heard her *scream*. You can't tell me that she's still out there."

"I'm sure she's not," Harrison said.

"Don't coddle me!" Stan said.

"I'm sorry," Harrison said. He surprised himself by sounding as sincere as he felt, or perhaps the reverse. "I shouldn't have said that. I just . . . I don't know if any of these things obey the same rules we do."

"But that's what you're here for," Martin said. "You're the official dragon slayer."

"I'm here, in this group, because I *used* to think that was my job."

"Maybe it's all of your jobs," Jan said. "Each of you is on the hero's journey."

"Oh no," Harrison said. "Leave Joseph Campbell out of it."

"The Mormon guy?" Stan asked.

"Joseph *Campbell*," Martin said. "The monomyth? *Star Wars*? Damn it, Stan, read a book."

"It's a pattern you see in many myths," Jan said. "A hero leaves the everyday world, and crosses over into the world of the supernatural. He gains magical helpers, faces great trials, fights strange forces, and wins a great battle. Then he comes back to the normal world with a boon—a gift. A reward."

"That's not my story," Harrison said.

"Well *I* crossed over," Stan said. "And what reward did I get?"

"Knowledge," Barbara said. "We get to find out things that no one else knows. We get the gift of understanding."

"Screw that," Stan said. "I want my hands back."

Harrison was the first to leave the building, but he stood for a while, scanning the sidewalks. Barbara caught him loitering. "Can't fool me," she said. "You still want to rescue the damsel."

"But who's going to rescue me?" he asked.

She laughed, and said good night. After a few steps she turned and said, "I always meant to ask you, did you see the portraits it carved?"

"The Scrimshander?"

"I've seen photographs of some of the bone carvings," she said. "But I've never seen a piece in person."

"I found its lair once," Harrison said. "A cave set in a cliff. Half the time it was underwater, but we crawled in there once at low tide. He'd made driftwood shelves to hold them. It looked like a hobo art gallery."

"What were they like?" she asked. "The scrimshaw."

"Horrible," he said. "And beautiful. Every bone came from someone he'd killed, but the portraits themselves . . . Somehow he made these people seem *more* than lifelike. They were just lines etched in the bone, some crosshatching, not even any color. But still. You know how they say an artist can capture someone?"

She tilted her head, thinking this over. "Take care of yourself, Harrison."

Later, we would hear how Barbara spent her night. She had supper with husband and sons, and washed the dishes while the boys tussled in the yard. It stayed light so long in the summer. After a while she rounded up her sons and kissed them on the tops of their heads. Then she kissed her husband good-bye. "Don't forget their soccer jerseys are in the dryer," she said.

After that, details were sketchy. We know she arrived at her apartment and locked the door behind her. She filled the big clawfoot tub with hot water, and arranged the mirror over it. A chair was pushed close to the tub to act as a side table for her tools and supplies: the straight razor; the rolls of medical tape; the bottle of Vicodin. There were still plenty of pills left when they found her. She wasn't trying to knock herself out, just dampen the pain enough to let her finish the job.

It was time to claim the gift. To finally know. She removed her clothes and climbed into the bath.

Chapter 9

We. Such a slippery little pronoun. Who is in and who is out? If we say, "We lost one of us," the number included in the pronoun changes in midsentence. To Martin the word was like a variable in a computer program, a running counter that had a different value depending on when you looked at it. But the problem was more difficult than that; the definition depended on who was doing the counting.

Did Barbara consider herself one of us, those last few weeks, that last meeting? Perhaps she was already watching us from the outside, a soldier spending her last night in the trenches, or a terminal patient sitting through her final Thanksgiving meal. We who remained didn't know what to think. How had we missed the signs? She seemed to be getting happier. Finally letting go of the damage the Scrimshander had done to her. Only in retrospect did we realize that it was the opposite. She was ready to embrace what he'd done to her.

Martin first understood this at the wake, when Harrison leaned in and said quietly, "Of course she was feeling better. She'd finally come to a decision." They were in line to greet the family, and Martin was pushing Stan in his chair. It was a very long line. Nothing brought out the crowds like an untimely death.

Barbara's husband and her two sons stood at the end of the line, greeting each visitor. The husband, a trim, balding man, seemed distracted. When someone was directly in front of him he would look baffled for a moment, and then automatically shake hands and try to say something. His attention, however, always flickered back to his son. The older boy stood beside him, the younger sat on a high wooden stool. They followed their father's example and shook each hand dutifully.

Behind the family was the pearl gray casket. Martin thought, Thank God it's closed.

After they made it through the line, Harrison started to say good-bye to them, and Stan said, "We'll sit over there." He pointed toward Dr. Sayer, who sat on a half-empty pew. Harrison exchanged a look with Martin, but followed them.

Martin parked Stan at the end of the pew. The doctor moved over to make room for them, and seemed grateful that they'd come. She clutched a clump of tissues and didn't seem to be done crying. Martin was shocked at this, then ashamed by his shock. Why was he surprised that she was human? Somehow he'd placed her in another category, the way little kids put teachers and pastors in a special category.

Yet, he still didn't know what to say. In desperation he said, "Is Greta coming?"

"I don't know," Jan said. "I tried to text her with the details, but . . ." She shrugged.

Martin looked at the doctor's long-fingered hands, which didn't seem to match her squat torso. She wore no wedding or engagement ring. It seemed that she'd come alone. There was so much he didn't know about her. Was it hard to run a therapy group without being able to talk about yourself, or was it a relief?

Stan said something that Martin didn't catch. "She shouldn't have listened to the whispers," Stan repeated. "You're not supposed to listen." He seemed to be offering this as advice to himself. Shit, Martin thought. Forty years and he's still not over it. And now Barbara, giving in some twenty years after her attack. Martin had been hoping that someday he'd stop imagining what the Dog Man had done to his roommates. That he'd forget that there were creatures that *right now* were clinging outside these stained-glass windows.

He'd told the group that he was adjusting to life without the frames, and some days he actually believed that. Mostly he ached to have them back. Therapy was about facing reality, and with the frames he saw *more* reality, and that was exactly what was driving him crazy. Pretending to be normal made life so difficult. So far he had not given in and bought a new pair of frames (it helped that he was broke). But what if he could never adjust?

He was fucked, that's what.

Greta appeared at the other end of the pew. She was dressed as always in black on black, but at least that was appropriate here. She sat down next to Harrison, and Martin thought, So that's back on. Or maybe not: Greta stared straight ahead, not talking. Harrison glanced at her, then seemed to give up. Despite the expensive midnight blue suit, he looked like he hadn't slept.

What a group. Sitting together at the funeral like a wing of the family. The psychiatric wing.

No, *I'm* not fucked, Martin thought. We *all* are.

Jan had decided not to follow the family out to the burial at the cemetery, and so had the rest of the group. They stood outside the funeral home making awkward small talk until Martin managed to load Stan into the transport. As they pulled away, Dr. Sayer said to Harrison, "I would like to ask a favor, but you must feel perfectly free to say no."

Jan had debated with herself about the ethics of even asking Harrison for help. His primary issue—besides the sense of deep alienation from humanity that every member of the group shared—was his self-image as a doomed captain. He felt responsible for others' lives, even as he was certain he'd fail them. Barbara's death was one more damning piece of evidence.

Harrison, however, was an expert in his field. And she needed his advice.

"What is it?" he asked Jan. He frowned. "Is it about Barbara?"

He was so quick. Jan touched her shoulder bag, but didn't open it. "I've gotten some pictures from the police. I'd like to have your opinion on them. Now, if that's possible."

Harrison glanced over his shoulder. Greta hovered twenty feet away. Waiting for him.

"Greta can come too," Jan said. "But she may not want to see them."

They walked a block to a small park and found a bench. Jan sat beside Harrison, while Greta stood by nervously, hands in pockets. "Barbara wasn't found immediately," Jan said. "The police think that by the time her husband got into the apartment, she'd been dead at least twenty-four hours."

"You talked to the *police*?" Greta said.

Jan realized that what she meant was, You talked to the police about *us*?

"Before I met with them and told them anything, I got permission from Stephen, Barbara's husband. Client confidentiality still holds for me, even after death." Jan lifted her iPad from her handbag and turned it on. "I wouldn't share these if I didn't think it was vitally important."

Greta moved behind Harrison's shoulder. Jan watched their faces as Harrison flipped through the pictures.

"The detective told me he'd never seen anything like it," Jan said. "She'd cut open each thigh without breaking a major artery. Then she'd had the strength to cut open her left arm along the bicep. She tried to cut the right arm too, but she couldn't hold the razor with her arm damaged like that."

They came to one of the worst pictures and Greta turned away. Harrison took a breath.

"The police just gave these to you?" he asked.

"The detective owed me a favor," Jan said.

Harrison said, "I don't see how I can help you with this. It looks like she cut along the scars she showed us. Re-creating what the Scrimshander did to her."

"She's not re-creating anything," Jan said. "Keep going."

After the crime scene pictures were the autopsy

pictures. "I told them to take these pictures. They didn't want to. They didn't know her history, didn't have her on file. I shouldn't have been surprised—she was attacked so long ago, in a different state. I told them to Google her maiden name. Then they understood."

The first several pictures were too messy to make much sense of; it wasn't clear which limb, which wound was being photographed. In each of them, though, white bone glinted from between the tissue.

"Fuck," Harrison said. "She was trying to see them."

"Yes."

He stared at the screen. "That last meeting, she asked me if I'd seen the scrimshaw. I said it was beautiful."

"Oh please," Greta said to Harrison. "She had this planned for a long time. One comment didn't send her over the edge."

Jan said, "I didn't bring you here just to see the wounds." She took the tablet from him and flipped ahead. "I asked the police to take pictures of what the Scrimshander had carved into her. I wanted them to open all the scars, but they wouldn't do that. The family would have a fit. So, we just have whatever Barbara got to. Here's the first image, from her left humerus."

The photo was at high zoom. The actual size of the etching was about an inch wide and four inches long, stretching down the bone. The picture was a bit hazy: the head and torso of a man, looking up and to his left. A crosshatch of curved lines radiated from him. The next picture was an even tighter close-up of the face.

"What the fuck?" Harrison said.

"That's you," Greta said, amazed.

It was Harrison. Not as a boy, but as he was now. He even seemed to be wearing a suit jacket, his uniform for the meetings.

"How is that possible?" Greta asked. "The Scrimshander drew this, what, twenty years ago?"

"Barbara was nineteen," Jan said.

Harrison flipped to the next image, and the next, each one an alternate shot of his portrait. Then he reached the first photo of the next series, Barbara's left femur.

Greta stepped back, her hand covering her mouth.

"I know, I know," Jan said.

"I was a kid when he did this!" Greta said. "How could he—?"

There were two figures in the picture. One was of Greta, crouching, holding what looked like a thread in each hand. The other was of a young girl, who stood with her hand on Greta's shoulder.

"That younger girl—is that you?" Harrison said.

"I thought it might be a before and after picture," Jan said.

Greta shook her head. "No. That's not me."

"But look at her neck," Harrison said. "She's scarred like you."

"I told you, that's not me."

Curved lines, similar to the background in Harrison's portrait, radiated behind the two figures. The threads in Greta's hands seemed to be the same width as the lines in the background, giving the impression that the hatchwork was not mere decoration, but something three-dimensional, like a net, or the rigging of a pirate ship.

"There's more," Jan said. "Martin is there, wearing the frames. And on her right arm, where Barbara stopped, there's a part of a wheel visible. I think it's Stan's wheelchair."

Harrison jumped up from the bench. "I hate this shit!"

"It's prophecy," Greta said.

Harrison wheeled about. "No! This is just . . . time shit. Time isn't running parallel on the other side. The two universes bump up against each other. You get thin spots at random places. Space, time, it's all different parts of the same bubble. Sometimes they look through and they see the future of our side. And sometimes we see the future of theirs."

"That's what prophecy is," Greta said. "Seeing the future."

"That doesn't mean it *has* to happen," Harrison said. "It's not predestined."

"You're lying to yourself," Greta said. "Listen to what you were just saying. The bubbles intersect. What they see has already happened. We just haven't got there yet."

"No, that's not how it works," he said. "There's still free will and—"

"You can't stop it!"

Jan stood up. "Greta, Harrison, please."

Greta growled and threw up her hands.

"Please," Jan said. "This may be important. We don't know what the Scrimshander's drawings mean, but Barbara thought he'd left her a message. She died to see it. That's what I would like to figure out now."

"Okay, we need all the pictures," Harrison said. "We need to see everything the Scrimshander put on her."

"We don't have that," Jan said. "The Scrimshander cut into Barbara in five locations. We have only three places Barbara was able to get to—three and a half perhaps, counting the glimpse of Stan. And we already know that x-rays and MRIs don't work."

"Then what do you want from me?" Harrison asked.

Greta started to say something, then shook her head.

Jan said, "I was hoping you could see something in these pictures that I didn't. You've dealt with the Scrimshander. You've dealt with . . . lots of things that I haven't."

"Okay," Harrison said after a moment. "Email them to me and I'll take a look."

Jan reached into her bag and fished out a small white thumb drive. "They're all on here. High-res."

Harrison took it from her. "And what if you don't like the message?"

"Oh, I'm pretty sure it's not good news."

Greta said she knew nothing about computers, and seemed content to walk around Harrison's apartment while he fiddled with his laptop. He paged through the pictures again and again, but kept coming back to the collection of portraits: of himself, Greta and the young girl, Martin, and Stan—or at least that wheel that suggested Stan. He had to assume that Barbara's portrait was on her sternum, the only scar she had not opened. Would that have been the nineteen-year-old Barbara, or the forty-year-old woman they'd just buried?

He arranged the pictures according to their location on Barbara's body. Harrison on the left arm; Greta and the mystery girl below him on the left thigh, clutching those threads; Martin on the right thigh. They were all facing inward or upward, as if gazing at the last scar on Barbara's chest. There was not enough of Stan visible on the right arm to know where he was looking, but the orientation of the legs and wheel suggested he was looking at that blank spot in the middle of the table. Harrison wanted badly to know what was hidden there.

He kept poring over the pictures, looking for clues. It was evident that the crosshatching behind each portrait was not just decoration. Greta's portrait, in which she clutched those lines as if they were cables, proved that. The lines curved, and by fiddling in Photoshop he could imagine them meeting up at the center of her body, the same point in space where all the portraits were gazing.

"Holy shit," Harrison said. "It's a spider web."

Greta put away her phone and looked over his shoulder at the screen. "And we're all in it."

"Us, and that girl," he said. She could have been any age from seven to fourteen. "You don't have any idea who she is?"

She didn't answer. He started to turn, and she said, "Who's in the center of the web?"

"Barbara, I guess. I don't know."

Greta straightened. "You need the actual bones."

"Yeah," he said absently.

"You could go dig them up."

He turned in his chair. "What? No."

"She didn't get cremated," Greta said. "That's on purpose. She *wanted* us to dig them up."

"We are not going to go grave-robbing."

"It's not robbing if Barbara wanted you to have

them. She died to find out what was in there. You can't just pussy out of this."

He squinted at her and gave her a slight smile. "You keep saying 'you.' Not 'we.' Are you in the group or not?"

She walked to the window and pushed aside the curtain. "Jesus, Harrison."

"So what's the deal?" he said. "You've been gone for weeks. You haven't even called me. And now you're in my house."

"This is not what I planned for today," she said. "All this . . . photo stuff."

"What was on the agenda?"

"I came to thank you. For keeping my secrets." She looked over her shoulder at him. "You didn't tell them, did you?"

She was talking about the fire. "It's your story," he said. "Your choice about what to say or not say."

She let the curtain fall back. "But you figured out what really happened."

"They didn't fuck up the ritual," he said "Not completely. It worked in the end. The Hidden One got into you. How could it not? You were designed for it."

"The prettiest little bottle on the shelf," she said.

"There's another secret I've kept," he said. "This one from you."

"Oh?"

"I can read you. Those designs on your skin—they're not just pictures. It's a kind of language." He could see that she didn't believe him. "When I was a kid, I got . . . infected with something from the other side. It did something to my head."

"So now you can read their language."

"Kinda."

"And what do my scars tell you?"

"Warning. Danger. Keep out."

She nodded as if she suspected this all along.

"You're irresistible to the Hidden Ones," he said. "But once you have one inside you, you're a lockbox. A prison cell. And the warnings tell everybody else to stay away."

"You should listen to them," she said. She flicked a hand toward the laptop. "Look at the web. I'm tearing it apart. If I stay I'll kill you."

"That's not what those mean," Harrison said.

She shook her head. "Oh, Harrison. *You're* the optimist."

"Listen to me—"

"Martin was right," she said. "The Sisters had come back for me. I knew you'd figured that out."

"Aunty Siddra's group couldn't be the only one living outside the farm," he said. "Did you know they were following you then? Following us?"

"No!" she said. "I mean, they'd tried to reach me before. In New York. I moved and I thought I'd lost them. Then—I never intended for anyone to get hurt. Not even Martin. But they're so protective . . ."

"I'm surprised they haven't come after me," he said.

She looked up sharply.

"What did you do?" Harrison said. "Why didn't they come after me, Greta?"

"I made a deal," she said.

He got up from the chair. "You're not supposed to make deals with the devil."

"But that's what I was raised to do. It's all I ever wanted to do—clinch that deal." She turned back to the window and moved the curtain aside. "Growing up, I prayed every day to be worthy of a Hidden One. Regular men were abusers or liars or . . . useless. But these creatures were divine beings. Cousins to angels."

She pressed her forehead to the window. "But then, when it finally entered me, I realized it wasn't divine at all. It was nothing but rage and *need*." Her voice resonated strangely against the glass. "It *hated* me. It hated Aunty Siddra. All of us. And I thought, Everything I've suffered, the years of pain, all that was to make a home for *this*? To put this sick thing inside me, just so it could walk around in our world?

"My holy purpose was a sham. My *great honor* was to keep this thing inside me like a loaded gun. I wasn't a bride, I was a receptacle. A fucking missile silo.

"I'd been such an obedient girl. Such an idiot. And

that moment I did what I had never done before. I said no. I cast it out of me, and I said, Do what you want."

Greta said nothing for half a minute. Harrison took a step closer. The streetlights made her face glow, and when she opened her mouth it seemed to be her reflection that spoke.

"Aunty Siddra burned first. She went up like kindling. And then the other women inside the bus, the dark-haired women who'd come with her. I walked down the steps to the yard. I was only a dozen feet away when the gas tank blew, but I was unharmed. Metal and glass flew around me, but the Hidden One kept it all from touching my skin.

"I turned to watch them burn. And you know what?" She kept her eyes pointed down, into the street. "I liked it."

Harrison said nothing.

"But my *mate* wasn't done yet. There were so many Sisters in the yard, crying or bleeding from the explosion. He started . . . *jumping*, from woman to woman, lighting their clothes on fire. He landed on the roof of the farmhouse and set the shingles on fire, then leaped over to the next camper. Hopping and skipping through all our crappy, makeshift homes. Dancing around me with joy in his molten heart. He didn't hurt me. He loved me now, because I'd set him free.

"Then I heard the women. It was like waking up.

You know how when you're first coming awake, there's nothing but silence? But then you wake up a little more and you can hear a radio playing in another room, the sound of voices? Suddenly I could hear the screams. Women were burning all around me, and burning alive inside the house. One of them was my mother."

Harrison took another step forward, and she put out her hand.

"Then it came to *me*," she said. "The Hidden One. It wanted more." She shook her head. "If I hadn't been raised like I was, if I hadn't spent most of my life in pain and under the knife, I might have been overwhelmed. But I'd learned detachment, right? Control. So I spoke to it. I said to him, There's a place I want us to go. But we can't go like this. Come to me. Hide inside me." She shook her head. "I don't think they understand humans. It loved me, and I'd just done this wonderful thing for it, so it believed me. It slipped down my throat. I could feel it churning inside me. Eager."

"I'm so sorry," Harrison said.

She seemed not to hear him. "When it was inside me, I sealed myself shut. I didn't need the final mark on my forehead. I could hold it in through force of will. *I* was the cork."

She turned from the window. "Oh, it howled. It hasn't stopped since."

"We can fix this," Harrison said.

"There's nothing to fix," she said. "Barbara and I understand that. The Sisters aren't going to stop. I just have to do what I was born to do." She tilted her head almost apologetically. "I'm their queen. They want me to lead them."

"That's the deal?" Harrison asked. "To go *back* to them? Greta, you can't do that. You don't have to protect me. Protect the others. We can figure out a way to get them to back off."

"I have to do this."

"*No*. There's no such thing as fucking destiny. We've talked about this."

"They've got a new bottle, Harrison. If I won't serve, they've got someone who will."

And then he got it. "The girl. You know who she is."

"Her name's Alia. She's younger than I was when I went up."

"Fuck."

"Yeah." She glanced back toward the window. "I've got to go now."

The whole time she'd been telling him her story, she'd been watching for them to arrive. "Are they out there?" he asked.

She started toward the front door. "I'm just so tired, Harrison. And they're going to stay after me until I give in."

"You can't respond to this," he said. "They're just using the girl like a hostage. Let me think. Maybe we can . . . I don't know. Something."

She stopped. Her smile was wistful. "You know, I kept thinking you were going to solve my problem for me. You're the monster killer. The hero. But I guess . . . kids' books, right?" She shrugged and continued toward the door.

He grabbed her by the elbow—and jerked his hand back. It felt as if he'd grabbed a hot steam pipe.

"It's okay," she said. "I've thought this through. I've got one play."

Pain throbbed in his hand and radiated up his arm. The skin, however, looked normal. Did he need ice, or was this some kind of psychosomatic shit?

She unlatched the door and opened it. Two women stood in the hallway. One of them tall, almost six feet, with thick dark hair like a Cherokee. The other was shorter, and wore a kind of scarf sweater that covered her head. Her lips were a shade of bright pink.

"Get the fuck away from her," Harrison said to the women.

The one with the covered head raised her arm. She held a small black pistol that seemed enormous. He felt as if he was hurtling into that black barrel.

The woman's pink lips parted as if in satisfaction.

He tried to settle himself. He'd had firearms

pointed at him before. But maybe this was one of the things you never got used to.

The tall woman took Greta by the arm and led her out. The small one kept her gun on Harrison.

Greta looked over her shoulder. "Good-bye, Harrison Squared."

Chapter 10

We were a team of professional insomniacs. Once you *know* there are monsters under the bed, closing your eyes becomes a foolhardy act. So, we paced. We stared into the dark. We listened for the creak of the opening door.

Dr. Sayer was no exception. Sleep had always been hard to come by for her, but the situation had only gotten worse since Barbara had died. In those thin hours after midnight, Jan was certain she'd made a terrible mistake. If she hadn't formed the group, if she hadn't prodded and poked them into *sharing* and *reflecting* and *processing*, perhaps their sadness would have gone dormant. Perhaps Barbara would still be alive.

If her patients had started talking like this she would have known what to say. So, on those sleep-starved nights, she said those words to herself, and sometimes believed them. Then she would head down to the basement. The relief didn't last long, though. Sometimes it vanished before she made it to the bottom of the stairs. Then she would walk back up, lock the door behind her, and make another circuit of her house.

Harrison had been right; this was no hero's journey they were on. Campbell didn't understand the other stories in the world. The group knew the truth:

A monster crosses over into the everyday world. The mortals struggle and show great courage, but it's no use. The monster kills first the guilty, then the innocent, until finally only one remains. The Last Boy, the Last Girl. There is a final battle. The Last One suffers great wounds, but in the final moment vanquishes the monster. Only later does he or she recognize that this is the monster's final trick; the scars run deep, and the awareness of the truth grows like an infection. The Last One knows that the monster isn't dead, only sent to the other side. There it waits until it can slip into the mundane world again. Perhaps next time it will be a knife-wielding madman, or a fanged beast, or some nameless tentacled thing. It's the monster with a thousand faces. The details matter only to the next victims.

As for the Last Ones, the survivors of each spin of the wheel, the best they could hope for was to learn how to live with their knowledge. On most days, she believed she could help others do that.

Deep into the night, however, the doubts slid their claws into her brain, pried her open like an orange. She feared that she was keeping secrets from herself. What if she was hurting these people? What if she longed for destruction? What if she'd become, at last, her mother's daughter?

And so it was almost a relief when the phone rang.

"Dr. Sayer," Harrison said. "I need your help."

Harrison was surprised to find Dr. Sayer waiting for him on her front porch. She was wearing black jeans and a thin black fleece over a flash of red T-shirt. Her hair was pulled back tight. It was weird to see her in street clothes. He felt like a third-grader spying his teacher at the grocery store.

She climbed into the car and he said, "You don't have to do this. You could just make the call, then stay here."

"It'll work better if I talk to him."

He had to admit that if *he* asked Martin, the kid would say no. "Okay," he said. "He never liked me *or* Greta. But he listens to you."

"Martin was *afraid* of Greta," Jan said. "He always liked her. He's made great strides. What did you do to your hand?"

"Nothing." He'd wrapped his hand with a beige chamois cloth he kept in the glove box. His skin still throbbed. "What's Stan's address?"

She read it off to him, and he typed it into the GPS. While he drove, she called ahead to Stan's house. He picked up immediately, and Harrison could hear his voice booming over Jan's cell phone.

"Could you wake Martin?" she asked Stan. Then: "Oh. Good." And then: "I don't know why, exactly." She looked at Harrison. "Harrison said we need Martin's skill set."

She told Stan a little bit of what Harrison had told her. She said to Harrison, "Martin wants to know if you have the frames."

"Tell him it's all set. Just get ready."

After she'd hung up, Jan said, "You do have a plan, right?"

"It's a *kind of* plan," he said. After the Sisters took Greta, he followed them downstairs, hanging back to avoid being seen—and shot. By the time he reached the street, they were pulling away in an ancient silver Pontiac, a wide, rattling thing. He ran back to the garage and to his car, but by the time he pulled around front the streets were empty. He swore at himself, then drove to Greta's apartment, not because he thought they'd be there, but because he couldn't think of anyplace else to check. Finally he called Jan.

Stan's house was a two-story Victorian guarded by a chain-link fence. The house seemed to have vomited its contents into the front yard. Furniture and objects loomed mysteriously out of the dark.

"Whoa," Harrison said.

"I really should do home visits," Jan said.

The front door opened, and Stan appeared in his chair, with Martin behind him. Martin pushed him down the ramp into the yard. And Stan, that crazy bastard, had a shotgun across his lap.

Harrison hopped out of the car and went to the gate. "No no no no no."

"What?" Stan asked.

"We just need Martin," Harrison said. "And no . . . that."

"You're going after crazy cult members," Stan said. "Trust me, you need artillery."

"We are *not* shooting anyone," Jan said.

"What are you going to do?" Stan asked. *"Talk?"*

Harrison noticed that Stan was wearing a pair of split-hook prostheses. "Wait, when did you get those?"

"I've got loads of 'em," Stan said. "Hooks, rubber hands, you name it. I only use them for special occasions. Like pulling triggers."

"Jesus," Harrison said. "Martin, get in the car. I'll get Stan back into the house."

"No," Martin said. "Stan comes with."

"Absolutely not."

"We discussed it," Martin said. "Stan's part of the group too. And I need him if we're going to do this. It's all for one—"

"Or all for nothing," Stan said.

Harrison thought about the images etched into Barbara's bones. All of them, connected. "Okay. Fine. But no fucking shotgun."

"You're going to regret it," Stan said, but allowed Martin to take the weapon from him. He waved to a spot in the yard and said, "Hide it in that oven there."

They managed to lift Stan into the backseat, and Jan helped buckle him in. Martin expertly collapsed Stan's chair and levered it into the trunk.

"You have the frames?" Martin asked. "I'll start loading the software."

"About the glasses . . ." Harrison began.

"You said you had a pair."

"We don't have time to go break into Radio Shack."

"They're not sold in—"

"It's going to be okay, Martin. Come on."

"How can I track them if you don't have frames!"

"Please, just get in."

Martin got into the front seat, and Harrison punched the accelerator. The streets were mostly empty of cars this time of night, though not necessarily empty of cops. He just had to hope they didn't get stopped.

"I *like* this car," Stan said from the back.

In ten minutes they swung into Harrison's neighborhood. His block was lined by boutique shops at ground level and upscale condos above. Harrison slammed on the brakes. Stan laughed throatily.

"There's the entrance to my building," Harrison said. "This spot is where they took off from, an hour and five minutes ago, give or take. What's your range, Martin?"

"I don't have a range," Martin said. "I need the frames!"

"No," Harrison said. "You don't."

"You have no idea how this works," Martin said.

Harrison opened the driver's side door. "Get out," he said to Martin. The kid looked at him. "Come on!"

Martin reluctantly climbed out of the car. Harrison took him by the shoulders and stood him in front of the headlights.

"You said Greta left trails wherever she went. Wakes, you called them."

"Yes."

"You know that those wakes can't be seen by the naked eye."

"That's why I need—"

"Listen to me!" Harrison said. It was difficult not to shake the kid. "Those trails are not made out of photons. Hardware can't see them. Software can't see them. Only *you* can see them, Martin. You want to know why?"

"This is bullshit," Martin said.

"You've got the sight," Harrison said. "The third eye. The sixth sense."

"I don't see dead people," Martin said.

"No, you see worse. I've met people like you before. You have a talent. You don't need a gadget to make it work."

"Is this where you tell me to put away the targeting computer?" Martin asked.

"No, I'm not—yes. Yes, this is where I tell you to put the fucking computer away. Use the force, Luke."

Jan had gotten out of the car. "What's going on?"

Harrison turned Martin to face the road. "They drove off in this direction. You see the intersection? Just tell me—did they turn left, right, or go straight?"

"I don't see anything."

"Concentrate," Harrison said. He gripped the kid's shoulders as if he were prepping him to go into the ring. "Picture the wake."

"I'm concentrating." Martin stared down the street.

"Left?" Harrison said. "Right?"

Martin wheeled and pushed Harrison's arms off him. "I *told* you, I need the frames!"

"Martin," Jan said softly. "Can we try something?"

Harrison put up his hands and stepped back.

"Just guess," Jan said to Martin.

"What?"

"Don't try to see the wake. Just look down the road and say the first thing you think of."

Martin took a breath. He squared his shoulders, stared at the intersection, and said, "Straight."

"Good," Jan said.

"Or maybe right."

"No take-backs. Ready? Into the car."

Harrison eased them up to the intersection. "Keep going?" he asked.

Martin shook his head. "I can't see a thing."

Jan was leaning between the front seats. "Doesn't matter. Keep going."

Harrison scowled at Jan, but he wasn't sure she saw his expression. He went straight, then slowed at the next cross street. Martin sighed, so Harrison kept going.

The light at Madison was red. Martin rubbed at his face. When the light turned green, Harrison accelerated, and Martin said, "Oh."

"What is it?" Jan asked.

"Nothing. Just . . . maybe we should have gone right."

"Harrison?" Jan said.

He wheeled the car around in the middle of the street. An oncoming car blared its horn and Stan raised a hook—flipping the metal bird.

At the light Harrison swung left onto Madison in the direction Martin had maybe kinda sorta thought they should go. Maybe, Harrison thought, we should just turn off the GPS and get a Ouija board.

"You're doing great," Jan said.

"Damn straight he is," Stan said.

Martin grew more confident in his answers. He led them crosstown, then south. The Sisters, if Martin's tracking was accurate, had stayed off the interstate and major throughways, but neither were they dodging or weaving. They probably never thought they could be followed.

Martin led them into one of the rattier sections of town: weather-beaten apartment buildings, check-cashing stores, '60s-era brick ranches defended by sagging chain-link fences. The cars at the curb were either gleaming refurbs or rusting heaps, a binary distribution.

Martin pointed at a space between buildings. "Turn right there."

"That's an alley," Harrison said. "But okay."

He nosed the car into the alley. He drove slowly for a hundred yards, and then Martin yelled, "Stop!"

The kid's eyes were wide. He was staring at the back of a three-story apartment building that looked like it had been abandoned years ago. "Can't you see it?" he said. "Up there."

Graffiti swirled like kudzu up the brick walls. The windows were covered with plywood except for the top floor, where lights flickered from an open window.

Harrison edged the car forward. Behind the building, three cars were crammed into a tiny gravel lot. One of them was the silver Pontiac the Sisters had driven away in.

"It's coming out," Martin said. His voice sounded far away. "The bottle's open."

The bottle's open.

Harrison swore. They might already be too late. "Okay," he said. "Everybody stay in the car."

"I'm coming with," Jan said.

"You're not leaving me out of it!" Stan said.

"Nobody fucking move!" Harrison said, not quite yelling. "I'll be right back."

He ran for the back steps of the building. There was a rear door, made of rusting metal. A chain and padlock held it closed.

He heard voices and looked up. From the open windows, female voices chanted in a strange language. Chanting was never good.

Jan appeared behind him. "I'm going around front," he said. "Just . . . guard this door." Before she could argue with him, he jumped off the steps and ran for the side of the building. The space between buildings was narrow and dark, the walls seeming to pinch shut above him. He bashed his knee against a hunk of metal—an air-conditioning unit? a refrigerator?—and stifled a shout of pain. He squeezed past the obstruction, then hobbled toward the mouth of the little alley.

A group of people was walking down the sidewalk toward him. He stepped back into the shadows, but really the whole street was in shadow: The sky above the rooftops was the color of a bruise; the sole patch of light glowed from a distant streetlamp. Three women, silhouettes in long skirts, passed within feet of him, talking in low voices. Arabic? Persian? He couldn't tell.

Wood shrieked. He risked a peek around the corner. The front door of the building was a wooden slab that looked like it had been chewed off at the bottom. A wedge of light spilled onto the sidewalk, then vanished as the door closed with another shriek. He waited ten, perhaps twenty seconds, then limped toward the entrance.

The door did not quite meet the frame. He leaned closer, but could see nothing on the other side but a dim light. He could not hear the women's voices, or the chanting he'd heard earlier.

Greta was wrong about him. He'd never been brave, even as a boy. Everything he did felt like a forced move, the only option he could think of at the time. And now here he was again, creeping around in the dark, playing Monster Detective.

He put a palm against the door and pushed.

The lobby was lit only by an electric lamp that sat on the floor. Rows of metal mailboxes gleamed along one wall, some of them open like black mouths: eels waiting in the rocks. A door once guarded the stairwell, but that was off its hinges now and lay flat on the garbage-strewn floor.

He'd stepped three feet into the lobby when a figure came down the stairs: the tiny woman in the sweater scarf. Her pink lips opened in surprise. They stared at each other for what seemed like seconds, but could only have been a moment. Then her eyes narrowed and her right arm jerked up. Her hand was full of metal.

He threw himself backward and slammed into the wooden door. It opened halfway and dumped him onto the cement. The Sister ran toward him, the pistol twitching at the end of her arm.

He scrambled backward. "Don't shoot!" Once, when he was younger, he would have been stupid enough to say something clever.

The Sister halted just outside the door, framed by the dim light of the electric lantern. She aimed the gun at his face. He was on his back, arms and legs splayed, a crab caught in mid-scuttle.

She glanced left, then right. He thought, Maybe there'll be bystanders! She wouldn't shoot him in front of witnesses, would she? But the street was as dark as before, and there was no one on the sidewalk.

"How the fuck did you find us?" she said. Her voice was nasal, the accent pure Brooklyn. That threw him. He was expecting something more exotic.

She took a step forward. "Talk, you piece of shit!"

The woman did not quite finish the word "shit." A black shape came out of the dark to her right and enveloped her, knocking her out of the wedge of light. The two figures hit the ground and rolled, then rolled again. The new attacker clung to the tiny woman's back.

It was Jan. One arm was cinched around the Sister's neck, the other around her chest and arm, pinning the gun to her side. Her legs were wrapped around the woman's hips.

The Sister tried to get to her feet; she got one hand under her and pushed, but Jan shifted her weight and rolled onto her back, keeping the woman pinned against her chest. The Sister struggled, but the choke-hold was unrelenting. The woman's pink lips worked as she tried to get air. The pistol dropped from her fingers.

Harrison reached them. "Jan," he said. "Dr. Sayer."

The doctor's face was distorted by some crazed emotion. The whites of her eyes had nearly vanished; her pupils were black and reflective as oil.

"Jan! Stop. Please."

The Sister had stopped moving.

Jan seemed to see him then. Her mouth went open

in surprise, and she pushed the Sister's body from her. "Did I—?"

He touched the Sister's face. "She's alive," Harrison said, though in fact he had no idea. He stared at Jan for a long moment, then held out his unbandaged hand. She took it and pulled herself up. Her strength was alarming.

In that moment several questions in his mind were answered, or rather became one answer, like notes resolving into a chord. He knew who she was— and who she used to be.

Perhaps she saw the understanding dawn on his face. "Not now," she said. "Greta."

They dragged the unconscious Sister into the lobby— Harrison thought it best to get her off the street—and then started up the stairs.

Their way was lit by fire. Every half-dozen steps sat a glass bowl filled with oil and a floating wick, but the inconstant light was almost worse than pure darkness; the stairs seemed to shift beneath Harrison's feet. Stabbing pain in his knee twice made him catch himself against the grimy walls.

Jan seemed to be having no trouble, though. She pushed past him, and he had to lunge after her to keep up. He felt like he was making a tremendous amount of noise, clumping up the stairs, huffing in the thick atmosphere of scented candles and stale urine.

At any moment he expected another Sister to appear, walking down to check on Pink Lips. He wasn't sure what Jan would do, or what he would do. He didn't know if he could cope with another gun aimed at his forehead.

On the second landing they heard the women's voices chanting above them. Jan threw herself up the remaining stairs. "Wait," he said, trying to keep his voice down, but she didn't seem to hear him.

He reached the third-floor exit. Jan was halfway down the corridor. At the end of the hall an open doorway quavered with candlelight. The singing was loud now, a chorus that made his skin itch.

Jan reached the doorway and stopped. Harrison caught up to her a moment later.

Everyone in the room had turned to look at them.

Inside were a dozen women, sitting or standing around an open space in the center of the room. The tall, Indian-looking woman who'd come for Greta stood there between two wooden chairs that faced each other. Greta sat in one, and in the other sat a young girl, perhaps eight or nine years old. Greta had stripped down to her wife-beater and boy shorts, and the girl was dressed similarly, in a white T-shirt and shorts. Her skin, too, was an echo of Greta's, their twin scars glowing and dancing in the flickering light.

Greta held the girl's hands in her own, and had been leaning toward her. Now they'd turned, like the rest of the women, to see who was interrupting them.

Greta looked at Harrison as if he was a stranger. No: an enemy.

"Don't do it," Harrison said. "Don't do it to her."

He'd had it wrong. He thought Greta was going back to the Sisters to be their queen. Instead she was going to pass her mate to the next bride in the list.

"Out," Greta said.

Jan said, "Greta, please . . ."

"Both of you," Greta said. "*Out.*" One of the women on the floor nearest them began to get up.

"OUT!" Greta shouted.

Then it was in the room with them: the Hidden One revealing itself, shuddering into the world. Someone screamed. Harrison threw up his hands to shield his eyes, but that was an animal gesture, useless against the non-light that burst from it. It was not a "fire creature." This was what fire aspired to. The heat that frightened the flames.

The thing churned toward them like a whirlwind. Harrison yanked Jan backward, into the hallway. The creature halted there on the other side of the doorway.

The door slammed shut. And then the women on the other side began to scream in earnest.

Jan shouted Greta's name. Harrison hauled her

back. The door shook in the frame; glowing holes popped through the surface like tiny meteor strikes.

"We have to get out!" Harrison shouted at Jan. "It's—"

The door exploded outward. Shards of blazing wood bit into his skin. He grabbed Jan's arm and yanked her toward the stairwell. Flames raced along the walls ahead of them. A roar filled his head, and he didn't know whether it was the sound of the fire or the voice of the creature.

The stairwell was clear. They threw themselves down the stairs, Harrison barely staying on his feet, tripping over the oil candles and sending tiny flames bouncing ahead of them into the dark. At each turning of the stairs they caromed off walls, slamming shoulders.

Then the fire found them. Flames rippled across the peeling paint, and in an instant the stairwell became a furnace. They ducked their heads and ran, Harrison keeping one hand on Jan's back, pushing her forward. Smoke jetted ahead of them. He could see nothing. He'd lost track of the number of floors. Somewhere above him, Greta's mate was burning down the house.

I've got one play. He'd misunderstood everything. First he thought she was going to be their queen, their Aunty Greta. Then he thought she was going to push the Hidden One into the new bride. But that wasn't something Greta could do. Not to another little girl. So she had to finish what she'd started years ago—and make sure the Sisters never did this to anyone else again.

Jan dropped to her knees, then reached back and yanked him down. "Stay low!" she shouted.

Jan crawled forward—but "crawled" was the wrong word. She scuttled forward, moving on palms and toes. And so *fast*. He'd never seen anything human move like that.

They were on a flat surface now. He kept falling behind and she would stop, reach back for him. Her hand would touch his face or shoulder, then she'd lurch forward again.

The smoke enfolded them. He could not see his hands, much less Jan. He was coughing, and his eyes were watering furiously. The heat was like a weight pressing him to the ground.

Jan stopped short, shouted something back to him. It took her several tries for him to understand that the way ahead was blocked. He crawled up beside her and touched hot metal: the building's rear door. The padlocked door. But how had they gotten back here? The lobby should have been right in front of them. Somehow they'd missed it, turned one too many times.

Jan started banging on the door. He joined her, hitting it with the side of his fist, but his blows were feeble. Then he started coughing, and suddenly he couldn't lift his arms. He dropped flat against the floor, trying to find oxygen.

So strange. All his life, he was sure he'd die in water. He'd nearly drowned when he was a toddler and had not gone back into open water until a very bad night in Dunnsmouth. Even after surviving that night, he'd never lost his certainty that the sea would eventually suck him into the dark. Death by fire had never occurred to him.

Jan still banged away. Or else someone else was banging to get in. Sorry, he thought. Come back later.

A rush of wind and heat blew past him. Then he felt hands on his arms, and he was dragged out of the building, into the parking lot.

"Hey, Martin," he said. Or tried to say. One breath and he was racked with coughing. Martin stood over him, still holding the tire jack, as Harrison rolled onto his side and attempted to hack his internal organs onto the gravel.

The building was in full torch. Every window blazed, opera boxes bursting with madly clapping flames.

"I could see Jan," Martin said. "Behind the door."

"Thanks," Harrison said. He raised himself to his elbows, coughed some more.

"But Greta . . ." Martin asked. "I think she's still in there."

Jan was sitting up a few feet away, looking at the building. Her eyes were shining. "Oh God," she said.

Harrison twisted to follow her gaze. The door they'd been trapped behind was wide open, the interior rippling with orange and yellow. A pair of figures walked down the corridor through the flames.

No, not *through*. The flames parted around them.

Greta and the new bride stepped out of the doorway, holding hands. They were untouched. Radiant.

A few feet from the door, Greta stumbled, then righted herself. The girl looked up at her, concerned.

Greta turned. The building seemed to swell with new heat like a great beast inhaling. And it *was* a beast. The creature proudly shook the walls, bellowing from every open window. So large! So mighty!

Then: An explosion knocked Harrison onto his side, shook the ground. Debris rained down. When he looked up again, the building was shuddering. Then, thunderclaps. Internal structures gave way as floors collapsed.

Greta and the girl were still standing, facing the building. Greta opened her arms.

Fire burst from every window. Rivers of flame bent through the air toward her and in an instant engulfed her.

He tried to shout, but his lungs had no air.

She blazed. She blazed, lost inside the fire. And then the fire was inside *her*.

Greta opened her mouth, and the flame glowed there. Her eyes were alight. The girl beside her cried out. Greta raised an arm as if to say, Just give me a second. Then she closed her mouth, and then her eyes. Sealing the bottle.

Greta fell over onto her side. Jan was beside her a moment later, kneeling on the gravel. "She's breathing," Jan called to him. He assumed that was the truth. Jan wasn't as much a liar as he was.

Behind him a voice said, "God *damn*." Stan was sitting on the hood of the silver Pontiac. With his shortened legs he looked like a little kid who'd been propped up there to watch the fireworks.

Harrison got to his feet. "God damn" pretty much covered it.

The little girl, the former bride, looked down at Greta, then back at the building. The fire still burned, but it was an ordinary fire now, feeding only on oxygen and fuel. Cremating the dead. How many of them had been this girl's family? One of them was likely to be her mother. And Greta—by releasing the thing inside her—had killed them.

The girl's expression was stony. Another sole survivor, he thought. Another victim. And another candidate for long-term therapy.

Sirens sounded in the distance. Harrison turned to

Martin and said, "You know how to drive?" His voice was a croak.

"Uh . . ."

"Start the car at least. The keys are in the ignition. And get Stan back in."

Harrison went to Jan and crouched down. "We have to get Greta and the girl out of here," he said. "I'll help Greta. Why don't you. . . ?" He nodded toward the girl.

Jan stood. "Tell me your name, child."

"Alia," she said.

"We have to go, Alia. Do you understand?"

She nodded. Jan held out a hand, but the girl declined to take it. They walked side by side toward Harrison's car.

Greta stared up at him. "Did I get them all?"

He looked at the building. "Pretty sure."

She took a breath. "Good."

He reached for her, hesitated, then touched her elbow. Her skin felt almost cool. She allowed him to help her up.

"You should go," Greta said. "Take care of Alia."

"There's room in the car for all of us."

"I'm a murderer," she said. "Again."

"Everybody falls off the wagon."

"Do *not* quip."

"Sorry," he said sincerely.

Martin was at the Pontiac, leaning over so Stan

could climb onto his back. Jan was leading Alia to Harrison's coupe. They had just reached the car when the door window shattered beside Alia's head. The girl screamed.

Another voice shouted. Harrison turned. A woman shuffled toward them. One leg dragged behind her, and what clothing remained seemed to be glued to her body. Most of her hair had been burned away, but he recognized her. She screamed again and raised her arm a second time. She was pointing straight at Alia.

He ran toward the shooter, trying to put his body between the weapon and the little girl. He heard the pop of the pistol, felt a sting on his left thigh that made him stumble.

He righted himself, threw open his arms, making himself as large a target as possible. His vision began to swim. The woman with the pink lips was ten feet from him. He doubted she'd miss from this distance.

When the next gunshot came, it was much louder than he expected. Then another shot, and another.

The woman leaned backward, and fell. She did not move.

Harrison pivoted, and his leg nearly gave way. "What the fuck, Stan?"

Stan was riding on Martin's back like a little kid. One hook steadied the barrel of a pistol; the other hook was looped around the trigger.

"I told you," Harrison said. He blinked to clear his head. "No . . . fucking. . . . " He began to tilt sideways, at first slowly, then very fast. He hit the gravel with a thump. His left pants leg was a very different color from his right, he noticed. Probably from blood. Almost certainly.

Jesus Christ, he thought. She couldn't hit the *plastic* leg?

He opened his mouth to complain, but words escaped him, and consciousness fled closely after.

Chapter 11

We met for the last time three weeks after the fire. One more session, though a secret one, off-site and off the books. No one wanted to get Dr. Sayer in more trouble than she was in already, and she wanted nothing more on the record for the patients. We were criminals now: murderers and kidnappers and conspirators. As a therapy group we had clinched the prize for Worst Outcome Ever.

We gathered at a breakfast restaurant a few miles from the Elms. Dr. Sayer knew the owners, and because at two in the afternoon the place was nearly empty, they gave her the run of the back dining room. Martin and Stan arrived early. Ten minutes after the hour Harrison came in on crutches, looking haggard.

"She's not with you?" Stan asked.

"Sorry," Harrison said. He took a seat at the table and set the crutches on the floor. "I think she's thrown away her phone. And no response on email."

"Nothing for me, either," Jan said.

The last time we had seen Greta was the night of the fire. She had volunteered to help Harrison check in at the emergency room. One minute she was beside his bed. The next she was gone.

Stan said, "You don't think she'd hurt herself?"

Jan shook her head. "I don't think so."

"She can't risk it," Harrison said. "If she breaks the bottle, it's not clear what would happen to the thing inside her. Maybe it goes into the little girl."

"But she couldn't even say good-bye?" Stan asked.

No one had an answer for that. Maybe we'd grown tired of processing these absences.

Harrison poured himself coffee from the thermos on the table. The silence went on. Jan, however, seemed willing to let them warm up slowly. Finally Harrison said to Martin, "New frames?"

Martin nodded and took off the thick glasses. "Sorry."

"No, it's okay. I'm just surprised."

"It's different now," he said. He turned the frames in his hands. "Before, I was afraid to take them off. Now I *want* to use them. For the boost." He smiled shyly. "I still don't understand what happened that night. How I tracked her. I was just guessing."

"But you weren't," Jan said. "Have you ever heard of blindsight?"

He shook his head.

"The brain knows more than it thinks it knows," Jan said. "The information you're processing isn't coming through your visual system. It never was."

"So these glasses are just props."

"What works, works," Stan said.

After a moment Harrison asked, "What happened to the little girl? Is she okay?"

"Alia's traumatized, but she's getting better," Jan said. She'd gotten the girl admitted to a short-term treatment center. After that, social services would take over. Jan was petitioning to become her supervising therapist.

"How'd you explain how you found her?" Harrison asked.

"I told them the truth—that I went to that building to help a patient in crisis. Then I saw the girl come out of the building."

"What about the other stuff?" Martin said. "What if Alia tells them everything?"

"Then she tells them," Jan said.

"You could lose your license!"

"What matters is the girl."

Harrison believed that was more true than she knew. If the group hadn't shown up that night, Greta would have still carried out her plan—but Alia, and probably Greta too, would be dead. And the Hidden One would be uncontained. He didn't know what that would look like.

"I believe Alia can come through this," Jan was saying. "I *know* others who have come through just as terrible beginnings. Scars heal." She smiled. "But at the moment I'm interested in hearing from you. When terminating a group, we'd usually have several meetings to discuss the process. I'm afraid we'll have to make do with this. So. Who's first?"

As if she had to ask. Stan launched into complaints about Martin. The kid was still living upstairs, for free, yet kept harassing him about the mess downstairs.

"Lately I've been thinking about fire safety," Martin said. "Do you know there's not even room for a bed in his bedroom? The frame is leaning against the wall! He has to strap himself in."

"Old habits," Stan said.

They went on like this for nearly ten minutes, with Harrison asking questions to keep them going. The argument meant nothing in the long run, and perhaps that was why it meant so much now. No one wanted to stop talking. No one wanted to terminate.

The waitress came by to take away the coffee thermos. It was clear they wanted the room back.

"How about you?" Jan asked Harrison. "Any thoughts about the group?"

"I did want to talk about one thing," Harrison said. He reached into the inside pocket of his suit jacket and dealt out the four 5x10 photographs. "These were taken during Barbara's autopsy," he told Stan and Martin. "It's the map the Scrimshander laid out on her body."

Martin and Stan leaned over the pictures, amazed. They hadn't seen them before.

"Us three, Greta, and the girl—Alia." Harrison said. "All bound up in the same web."

"I see it," Stan said quietly. "You see the lines?"

"Alia too," Martin said. "Weird."

"But there's a piece missing," Harrison said. "The Scrimshander left another portrait, on Barbara's chest. The forensic techs didn't open her up there." He put a finger down in the empty center. "Here"

"Who's there? Barbara?" Martin asked.

"That what I thought at first," Harrison said. "But Barbara's the canvas—in a way she's already there. It's someone else." He looked at Jan. She was staring at the table, holding herself still. Keeping control.

"You brought us together," Harrison said to her. "I think it's time to hear why you did that. Why you put yourself on the line for us."

Jan looked up. "I couldn't tell you," she said. "It wasn't ethical. The group is about you, not me."

"Wait a minute," Stan said. "What are we talking about?"

DARYL GREGORY

She began to tell them her story. Harrison had already figured out most of it, but Martin was amazed. Stan, for whom the story mattered most, was beyond stunned. He seemed to barely process the information.

Jan spoke for nearly a half hour. When she finished, she reached across the table and placed her hand on Stan's arm. "I have something to show you," she told him. "Something in my house." She looked up at the others. "Do you all have time for a short trip?"

Martin and Harrison carried Stan in his chair up the steps and into the house. Jan unlocked a door that led to the basement. She did not turn on the lights.

"I think Stan should see this on his own," Jan told them. "I can take him from here."

"Are you sure?" Martin said. "He's heavy."

"I'm stronger than I look," she said.

Jan levered Stan down a step, then two. Then she reached back and shut the door behind her.

Harrison and Martin exchanged a look, then went into the living room. After a while Martin said, "You're going after her again, aren't you?"

Harrison nodded.

"She's a mass murderer," Martin said.

"It's true."

"But *dozens* of people. She let that thing burn them."

Harrison sighed. "Yes."

"And she's still carrying the monster inside her."

"Still . . ."

"Yeah," Martin said.

They were quiet for a while. Then Harrison said, "The Scrimshander went to a lot of trouble to send a message to us."

"What's the message?" Martin asked.

"I don't know. The little girl's part of it, though."

"What?"

"I think there's something big coming."

"Jesus," Martin said. He took off the frames and pinched the bridge of his nose. "Is it ever over? Do we ever get to just . . . win?"

Harrison chuckled. After a moment he said, "When I was a kid I used to play soccer. This was in San Diego, before we moved to Dunnsmouth. It was this park district league, and they didn't keep score. Losing would be bad for self-esteem. So at the end of the season, every player got a ribbon. A blue ribbon, stamped in gold, that said 'Participant.'"

Martin looked at the glasses in his hand. "Fuck."

"Congratulations," Harrison said.

In the basement, Dr. Sayer and Stan had reached the cement floor. She still had not turned on the lights.

Stan stared into the dark. There was a familiar smell

in the dank air. His heart beat very fast. "You always took care of me," he said. "You were always so kind. None of the others—"

"I didn't stop them," she said.

"You were a child." He smiled. "The Pest. And all this time I thought you were a boy. You would climb up there with me . . ."

"I still have trouble sleeping," she said. "That's when I come down here." She stepped away from him, and then the lights came on.

"Oh," he said.

Along the far wall, scores of thick ropes formed a dense web that stretched from ceiling to floor and wall to wall. The ropes were tied into steel hoops that were bolted into the floor, the wooden joists, and the cinderblock walls. It was the Weavers' barn, in miniature.

"It's—" His voice broke. "It's perfect." He looked at her. "May I?"

She wheeled him to the web. He ran a stump along one of the ropes. Then he looked at her again and she nodded. She squatted in front of his chair, put her arms under his, and lifted him. Lifted him easily.

He placed one arm through a loop in the net. She hoisted him higher so that he could get his legs between the ropes. The web cradled him.

"Not too tight?" she asked.

He closed his eyes. "I should hate this," he said. "I should *hate* this. But . . ."

"It's okay," she said. "We're different from other people." She climbed up into the web, moving carefully to keep from shaking him. She slipped her arms and legs between the ropes and settled beside him, and whispered into his ear.

After perhaps an hour, Harrison and Martin heard the wheelchair thunking up the stairs. Jan emerged from the basement backward, pulling Stan after her. The old man slouched in the chair, looking almost drunk.

"You okay?" Martin asked.

"I napped," Stan said. "Best sleep I've had in years."

We said the things people always said, promising to keep in touch, making vague plans to meet again soon. We went to our homes congratulating ourselves on being a little stronger than before we met.

That was in daylight. By nightfall, our thoughts had turned to the promise written on Barbara's bones. We went about our evening routines, trying to think of something else. Harrison poured himself one last drink. Martin strapped Stan into his frame. Jan made her way down the stairs. And Greta, in some city unknown to the rest of us, locked the door of her hotel room.

Each of us, as we turned off the light, felt a tingle of dread.

But that was all right. The feeling was as familiar as the dark. Some of us thought of what Jan had whispered in the basement, words that Stan had repeated for the others as we said our good-byes. We're different from other people, she'd said. We only feel at home when we're a little bit afraid.

Daryl Gregory is an award-winning writer of genre-mixing novels, stories, and comics. His first novel, *Pandemonium*, won the Crawford Award and was nominated for a World Fantasy Award. His other novels include the Philip K. Dick Award finalist *The Devil's Alphabet* and *Raising Stony Mayhall*, which was named one of the best books of the year by *Library Journal*. His science-fiction novel *Afterparty* came out in April 2014.

Many of his short stories are collected in *Unpossible and Other Stories*, which was named one of the best books of 2011 by *Publishers Weekly*. The stories previously appeared in the *Magazine of Fantasy & Science Fiction*, *Asimov's Science Fiction*, and *MIT Technology*

Review Magazine, and in such anthologies as *The Year's Best Science Fiction* and *Year's Best Fantasy*.

Gregory's comics work includes the *Planet of the Apes* series, the *Dracula: The Company of Monsters* series (co-written with Kurt Busiek), and the graphic novel *The Secret Battles of Genghis Khan*. He lives in State College, Pennsylvania, where he writes programming code in the morning, prose in the afternoon, and comics at night.